CONTENTS

♦

The Hot Girl   5
Pluck It Out   19
Dust Particles   49
The Ryans   57
Roadkill   63

♦♦

Nicole Took Her Shirt Off First   73
The Other Time a Grown Man
    Threatened My Life   81
Automotive Safety   97
State of Emergency   111
Math Class   123

♦♦♦

I Am the Snake   137
Rational Fears for Only Children   151
Hazel: A Diptych   161
Same Person, Different Fires   189

◆◆◆◆

The Arsonist   201
Natural Selection   207
Little Bitch   211
Santa Muerte   225
Is It Jackal or Is It Dragon   237

Acknowledgments   239

YOU ARE
THE SNAKE

ALSO BY JULIET ESCORIA

Juliet the Maniac
Witch Hunt & Black Cloud: New and Collected Works

YOU ARE THE SNAKE
STORIES

JULIET ESCORIA

SOFT SKULL
NEW YORK

First Soft Skull edition: 2024

Library of Congress Cataloging-in-Publication Data
Names: Escoria, Juliet, author.
Title: You are the snake : stories / Juliet Escoria.
Description: First Soft Skull edition. |
New York : Soft Skull, 2024.
Identifiers: LCCN 2023053064 | ISBN 9781593767747
(trade paperback) | ISBN 9781593767754 (ebook)
Subjects: LCGFT: Short stories.
Classification: LCC PS3605.S36 Y68 2024 | DDC 813/.6—dc23/
eng/20231121
LC record available at https://lccn.loc.gov/2023053064

Cover design by Farjana Yasmin
Cover photograph © Alamy Stock Photo / foodfolio
Book design by Wah-Ming Chang

Published by Soft Skull Press
New York, NY
www.softskull.com

Printed in the United States of America

10 9 8 7 6 5 4 3 2 1

For Scott

YOU ARE
THE SNAKE

THE HOT GIRL

It wasn't as if there hadn't been signs. The first time, we were at the IHOP near the racetrack, Kat and Mark and my boyfriend Jim. We'd been at a party down the street and were now sobering up. Kat was my best friend, this girl I had nothing in common with. I'd known Mark since elementary school, my next-door neighbor until his parents got divorced. Jim was new. I'd rung him up at the grocery store and we'd spent most nights together ever since. I couldn't remember why we were laughing but things were funny. We were having a good time, my friends and my new boyfriend and me.

But then Mark mentioned a girl we'd gone to school with. She'd gone away to college and now had dropped out, moved back home. That was all he said. No commentary, no detail, just facts.

Kat was this wild beauty, angles and legs. Her hair was dark and her eyes were dark and she looked feral, all the time, even when she was happy. And when she wasn't. You didn't want to look, those brown eyes flashing to black discs like some lesser demon.

As soon as he mentioned her name, the college dropout, the mood shifted. Mark knew right away he'd fucked up. He put his hand over hers and she pulled it away. Jim already knew about Kat when she got mad. He made eye contact with the waitress and smiled and she brought us the check. Jim peeled out two twenties, said he didn't want change. He had a fancy tech job I didn't understand.

We headed out to the parking lot, Kat in front, beeping the fob to her new SUV. She'd crashed the last one. DUI. Rich daddy.

Mark was right on her heels and I could tell he was trying to figure out what to do. I looked back at Jim and knew that even though he was still drunk he was wishing he'd brought his own car. Mark tried to put his arms around Kat, but the moment he touched her, she whirled around, those black demon eyes. I saw something glint and then her hand was at Mark's hand and then he was yelling. I heard something clatter on the ground. It was a butter knife. Kat laughed and ran around to the driver's side and jumped in. She almost backed into Jim on her way out, so fast her tires squealed.

We stood there for a second and I looked at Mark's hand. It was fine, just a red dent in the palm and a tiny cut on the webbing. There was nothing to do but laugh. Kat had stabbed him with a butter knife she'd stolen from IHOP and then ditched us in the parking lot. But when we got in the cab I could tell Mark didn't think it was funny. "I'm done with her," he said, quiet like he was trying to convince himself. And for a couple weeks, he was, the longest stretch they'd ever broken up.

Kat and Mark had been back together for a couple weeks the night I went over to her mom's condo. We spent a lot of time over there. Her mom was never home. Supposedly she worked hard into the night, always up for some promotion. But really she was sleeping with her boss, a married fat man whose name was on the firm. Oftentimes she never came home at all. Less often, Kat woke in the morning to find his big Mercedes parked in their driveway.

Jim met us after he got off work. It was still light out. We already had the margarita mix and the ice and Kat's mom's fancy blender, so we sent him out for a handle of tequila.

We were one drink in when everyone started coming over, mostly people I'd known since high school. One of them was Becca, who'd only been around for a couple months. She had long blond hair, perfect tits, real pretty, but still she didn't compare to Kat. A million girls looked like Becca. I'd never seen anyone who looked like Kat.

The music was loud, stereo turned all the way up, bass beating the floors. Kat and Jim and I went upstairs to her mom's bathroom. Jim sat on the ledge of the bathtub, took out the cocaine. Kat handed him a big flat mirror and he started chopping with his credit card, so carefully that Kat and I grew impatient, crawling over the ledge like children into the tub. Kat curled in a ball, cheeks pink with tequila, and smiled at me, those otherworldly tiny white teeth. Her body tilted and she slipped, falling into me. We laughed, and she stayed there, her hair glossing like water across my legs. Then she grabbed my hands, squeezed them tight, and I felt the soft touch of her lips against my skin, prickling my whole body with some ice-cold feeling I couldn't name.

"I love you so much," she said. "Let's always be friends."

She was always doing that, this weird erratic emotional intensity that didn't seem real. I never knew what to say. So I just grabbed her hand back, two little squeezes, pulled my hand away and sat up.

Jim was still chopping the coke, which wasn't good, the kind I would have left in chunks. I felt a sharp pain on my leg and saw Kat's long polished nail pressed against it, hard. She turned her thumb, making an *X*.

"Mosquito bite," she said. "So it won't itch."

When I looked at my leg, there was no bite there, nothing except for Kat's *X*. But I didn't say anything. I snorted my lines.

When we left the bathroom, more people had arrived, including Mark. The three of us stood at the top of the stairs, surveying. Mark was sitting in the big stuffed chair in the corner, eyes down and face expressionless, completely out of place among the rest of our loud friends. Kat grabbed my hand again, her nails in my wrist, and I felt something inside her flicker. I looked at Mark again and realized the person sitting closest to him, on the couch, leaning over, cleavage spilling, was Becca. That was the first time that night I felt the bad thing, had the urge to leave, but I was too fucked-up and Jim was too fucked-up so instead I stood at the top of the stairs, away from it all, watching Kat go down and plop herself on Mark's lap, grab his face and kiss his mouth, prying his lips open with her tongue.

Jim was still standing behind me. "Let's smoke," he said, and we went downstairs and outside.

I think it was around two. Most of the people had left. I was on the patio with Jim and Kat and Mark. Mark was telling one of his long stories, making us laugh even though we'd heard it before. Kat was staring at him, that dumb adoring gaze she never shone on anyone else. Then Becca slid open the door. She didn't come outside. She just looked at Mark for a second and then she closed it.

Kat threw down her cigarette, ground it out with her pointy heel. Fuck-me boots. Here in her own house: a mini-skirt that showed her ass cheeks when she bent down, and those boots, pointy heels pockmarking her mother's white carpet. She reached for Mark's hand right when he brought the cigarette to his mouth. It looked like he was swatting her away but really he just didn't notice. He took a long drag before continuing his story.

Jim made a clicking noise with his mouth, trying to signal me to get back inside. But my cigarette was only halfway done and I was high as hell and wanted another.

"I'll meet you inside in a sec," I said.

"Okay," he said, his tone telling me I was making a mistake.

And I knew I was, but I'd seen it all before, Kat's drunken jealousy. The time she threw Mark's father's antique vase at his head and missed by a mile, the ceramic shards splintering all over the wall, raining on the carpet. I'd been in the back seat the time she threatened to crash us all into the concrete divider. Instead, she pulled over, right on the 5, told him to get the fuck out and walk home. It took a good twenty minutes for us to settle her down, and even when we were back on the road her hands still shook with rage. And, of course, the butter knife.

I could feel the anger coming off her, thick as walls. But Mark either didn't feel it or was pretending not to. He drew on his cigarette, went on with his story. Kat grabbed his hand, the same damn one. The cherry fell on the ground. Kat screamed, "You burned me!" Like it was all his fault and not hers.

"Jesus," Mark said. "What did you think would happen? You grabbed my cigarette."

Kat pulled out her hand, showing it to us under the patio light. "Look what you did," she said. There was a red ring on her palm, black with ash.

She opened the patio door, slammed it shut. I figured she was just getting some ice. But when I tried to open it a second later, it was locked. We were trapped.

"Jesus," Mark said again.

"You know how she is," I said. I didn't know why I was defending her.

"Oh," he said, "I know."

I heard a bang and turned around. Kat had opened the door. She was yelling, her wild hair falling all over the place, a fit of anger and expletives. She was holding something in her hand but I didn't stop to think about what it might be. She pushed Mark and he fell against the fence, knocking over a plant in its terra-cotta planter. It split open on the cement, the wet smell of dirt. "Kat, it's okay," I said. "Calm down."

Except Kat was still over him, still yelling, her arm moving toward him. There was a scream, this time Mark's. A metallic clatter on the ground. A knife. A bloody knife. She'd stabbed him. The split in Mark's jeans, and then blood.

I saw Kat's face, just for a second, frozen in a look of shock. And then she was gone, hopped right over the fence.

Mark was pale. His jeans were soaking up a lot of the blood but it was spurting pretty bad, a slow steady pulse matching the beat of his heart. I couldn't tell if I should tie something around his leg to stop the blood or call 911. A second later, Jim was out there, he'd heard the noise, and he was taking off his shirt and yelling at me to make the call. I ran into the house. Nobody else had noticed that anything was wrong. I grabbed the cordless.

The first thing the operator asked me for was the address, which I didn't know. I tried to find a piece of mail. She asked more questions. I tried to explain. I said something about my friend being stabbed, the blood, it was spurting. I described the neighborhood. I couldn't tell if I was making sense. I couldn't understand the questions. I found a Nordstrom bill on the kitchen table, read the address.

I looked at Jim through the glass, his hands bloody now, black blood on the concrete and the knocked-over plant. I couldn't see Mark, what was happening to him. The woman made me stay on the line. No, she wasn't armed. I told her about Kat and the fence, and the butter knife, the time on the freeway, I don't know why, and it seemed like all I could hear was my stupid voice and my own heavy breathing.

It only took a few minutes for the paramedics to arrive. They took Mark away on a stretcher. He didn't look good, blood all over and his face pale as a plate. The rest of us tried to figure out what to do, who could drive, where to go. I wanted to go to the hospital with Mark. But then the police arrived and told us we couldn't leave. They pretended not to notice the coke and the weed and the alcohol, only half of us old enough to drink.

They talked to me right away. I was wishing I had listened to Jim and come inside so I had less to say. The officer I was assigned was young and seemed stupid, like he was just pretending to be a real cop. I kept forgetting what he asked right after he said it. I told him everything I'd just said on the phone but he kept asking questions.

He wanted to know if I had any idea where Kat might have gone. I didn't want to be a narc but I couldn't get rid of the picture of Mark's face and all that blood. I told him about the people we knew in the complexes near Kat's, the pay phone in front of the movies, the park.

Toward dawn, we still weren't allowed to leave so I called Mark's father. He picked up right away, told me the news. Mark had flatlined at the hospital, a severed femoral artery. They sewed it up and transfused the blood. One of Mark's dad's friends had been on duty, he was lucky, one of the best surgeons in the state. I asked to talk to Mark but he was asleep. His dad's voice was cold, very matter-of-fact. He told me to go home, get some rest.

When the cops finally let us leave, it was light out. Kat's mom hadn't gotten home yet so we just left the front door unlocked. There was still blood on the patio but I told myself it wasn't my problem, wasn't my mess to clean up. Jim and I went back to his apartment. He didn't say anything, just took a shower and crawled into bed and went to sleep. I wondered where Kat was. I was wide awake and after a while of trying to calm down I just gave up. I smoked a cigarette, then another, thinking about calling Mark's dad again or Kat, but I didn't want to bother him and I didn't want to be a part of Kat's crime.

I was still awake when she called. I thought she'd at least call from jail but nope, just her cell phone. She'd run to the condo of a couple we knew down the street, which seemed dumb because they were more Mark's friends than hers and there was blood all over her hands. She laughed at that, like it was funny to show up at someone's house in the middle of the night covered in blood.

From there, she'd guessed that the police would be looking for her around the neighborhood, so she walked through town on side streets until she got to the beach. I was waiting for her to ask about Mark, what had happened, but all she wanted to talk about was how she'd gotten away, like she was some kind of badass, rather than a psycho who'd almost killed the person she loved. Supposedly.

"I hope my mom goes straight to work!" she laughed. "I need to clean up that mess."

"What?" I said. I couldn't believe that the thing she was concerned about was a mess.

"She's going to be so mad if she knows I had that many people over."

"Kat," I said, "Jesus fucking Christ." She must have thought it was like the butter knife, I figured. She must have been thinking she hadn't hurt him that bad. "He almost died. You almost killed him." I told her about the flatlining and the surgery and the artery. "It's the major artery in your thigh."

"I know what it is," Kat said, her voice tense for the first time the whole conversation. "I took anatomy."

"Anyway," she continued. "Can you pick me up?"

"Pick you up? And take you where?"

"Home," she said, like I was stupid. "I need to clean up."

"You almost fucking killed Mark."

Kat laughed at that. I guess she liked the idea of herself as an almost-murderer.

"Don't you feel bad?" I asked.

She was quiet for a moment, as though she was trying to figure out the safest thing to say. "It was self-defense," she tried out. "He burned me with his cigarette."

I remembered the legal shit she'd been steeped in her whole life, about not admitting guilt, bending the truth to best fit your circumstances, her sleazy mom and that fucking law office. She didn't feel bad. She couldn't.

I hung up the phone, annoyed to be on a cell, where all I could do was push a button rather than slam it into a receiver.

She left me a voicemail after she got out of jail, only one night, complaining and laughing about how it was shitty and dirty. I deleted it. A few days later, she left another, her voice cold, calculated, saying she was calling to see how I was doing. I deleted that one too. I'd just come back from seeing Mark at the hospital, twenty-seven stitches and a morphine drip. My mom asked where she'd been but I just said we'd gotten in a fight, couldn't bring myself to say it aloud. I went through my closet, my car, under my bed, searching for any trace of her. A T-shirt, mix CDs, several hair ties, her long dark hair still snarled on the elastic. Into the trash. Threw her away.

I never talked to her again. I thought maybe I'd have to testify in court, but Kat just pleaded guilty and they let her off with three years' probation. Almost killed someone, one night in jail. After that, a civil case. Mark won. He didn't get enough. There was the surgery and the recovery and the fact that he now walked with a cane. Kat's mom pretended to be a lowly law clerk, claimed that Kat's dad was out of the picture rather than living in some giant house in Tahoe with a boat. The judge believed her. The whole thing made me so sick, wondering what it all said about me. Nothing good.

Years later, I was taking Spanish at the community college. I'd finally transferred to a real university, was just getting my language requirement out of the way over the summer. And she walked into the classroom, beautiful and wild-looking as ever. She must have spent some time at the beach, or on vacation, her skin a perfectly glowing shade of golden. I tried to look away, pretend I hadn't noticed her, but our eyes locked and then she took a seat at the back of the classroom, pulled out a hand mirror, checked her lip gloss. It made me so angry when she introduced herself in Spanish—*Mi nombre es Kat y me gusta viajar y escuchar música*—her voice steady and clear, like the whole thing hadn't made the slightest dent on her life at all. *Su nombre es Kat y le gusta apuñalar a su novio*, I murmured, but nobody heard me but me.

I made sure to sit as far away as possible, and always glared and laughed when she presented to the classroom. It was the same Kat as always, coming into class each night in a full face of makeup and too-short skirts, the only incongruency in her perfect appearance that messy hair. A few weeks in, she stopped showing up, and I was hoping it was my fault, that my glares had finally gotten to her, that she finally felt the slightest bit of remorse, that stabbing Mark finally had some sort of tangible consequence.

But one day I got to school early, heard two boys talking, these two skaters who seemed dumb as fuck and no older than eighteen, the age I'd been when I met Kat.

"Where's the hot girl?" one of them asked.

"Which one?" his friend said.

"The *hot* one."

"Oh. That one. Yeah, I dunno."

I knew who they were talking about. Kat. "She's not hot," I said, my voice louder than I'd intended. "She's insane. She stabbed her ex-boyfriend for no reason. Went straight through his femoral artery, nearly killed him. He still limps."

The two boys looked at me, and then each other.

"That's so hot," one of them said.

"Super hot," the other one said. "I need her number."

Then they laughed.

PLUCK IT OUT

I.

I got my first period the same day as the hailstorm. I was in the library with my English class, looking at the biographies, when I felt something hot and globby exit my body. I wasn't friends with Rachel yet. I wasn't friends yet with anybody. I'd just transferred to New Valley Christian, in the middle of the school year, my parents fed up with my "behavioral problems." Really all that had happened was I was sent to the principal's once and I got a D on a math test and suddenly there I was at NVC, no friends, being forced to pray while wearing a uniform. Rachel wore her pleated skirt hemmed above her knees with Doc Martens, just like me, so I asked her to come with me to the bathroom.

I shut the stall door behind me and pulled down my underwear. The blood was shiny and thick like snot. I felt a sharp twist in my gut. Menstrual cramps. So this was what they felt like.

"I started my period," I said to Rachel on the other side of the door. I rolled some toilet paper and stuck it in my underwear.

"Is it your first time?" Rachel said.

"Yeah," I said. "I don't have anything."

"I have a pad in my bag," she said. "But it's in the English room."

We asked Mrs. Lilly if we could go back. She didn't want to let us but Rachel told her it was "woman trouble" and Mrs. Lilly cleared her throat and then said we could go.

It was raining that day. It'd been raining all week, El Niño. I'd lived in California for seven years at that point and it seemed like it was always El Niño, endless rain every winter. We pulled up the hoods of our NVC sweatshirts and ran into the rain. The pavement was pocked with puddles and we stomped our boots in them as we ran, water splashing our legs, laughing like maniacs.

We were halfway up the hill when I felt something hit my arm. The ground was sprinkled with what looked like gravel. I stopped for a second, picked up one of the tiny pebbles. It was cold and wet. "What is that?" I said to Rachel, holding it out in my palm. But then more started falling and it stung through my sweatshirt. We started running again, the pebbles pelting the backs of our legs.

We made it back to the classroom just when the hail started to get big, the size of coins, ugly and gray. We stood in the doorway of the classroom, watched the rocks fall from the sky, smacking the palm trees and benches, piling on the grass. "Wow," I said.

"Is that hail?" Rachel said. Water dripped from her boots and her nose.

"I think so," I said.

The hail drummed on the metal roof of the English room, which was really a trailer. I felt powerful, as though I'd shaped it, glued the blood and the hail together into a new chaos. A pulse throbbed between my legs, my heart beating hot in the thick vein of my throat.

Rachel got the pad out of her bag and it was pink and crinkly. The bathroom was across the courtyard and it was still hailing, so I asked Rachel to turn her back. I pulled down my dirty underwear in the middle of the English room, wrapped the wings around the way the PE teacher had shown us in fifth grade. The toilet paper was bloody. I crumpled it in a piece of notebook paper and threw it in the trash.

The hailstorm gave us an excuse to not go back to the library. We took off our wet sweatshirts, got paper towels from the sink, and wiped the rain from our faces. I rubbed off a smudge of mascara from Rachel's cheek with my finger. I smelled her smell, Calvin Klein perfume and rain and sweet sweat. We sat on the ground and talked until lunch. That was how we became friends. Later I learned the last time it hailed in San Diego was thirteen years ago, the same year we were both born.

II.

I spent the night at Rachel's house that weekend. She had two houses: a condo with her mom and a big house on top of a hill with her dad, a doctor. That weekend, it was the big house.

Her dad came out to the driveway to meet my mom. He was handsome in a dad way and his blue eyes were icy cold. The parents said hi and my mom drove off. He handed Rachel a twenty and said we could order pizza. We went back in the house and I didn't see him for the rest of the night.

Rachel had her own TV, a big beanbag chair, and a four-poster bed. She turned on MTV. It was playing a rap video. Rachel knew all the words, rapped along quietly. I knew the words too but I didn't say them. She said the curse words louder than the rest, the *bitches* and the *asses*, and with this I felt a jangly part of myself settle.

I'd felt so out of place the entire month at NVC. I wasn't a Christian. My family was technically Catholic, but my parents had raised me as nothing, and they laughed when I thought Jonah and the whale was the same story as Pinocchio. I didn't know anything about Adam or Eve or original sin, had never thought much about hell or the meaning of Christmas. But now I was surrounded by people who believed in this hero named Jesus. They prayed every night and spent Sundays at church. I'd been to church exactly once in my life, when my grandma died, and the only Bible

I'd ever seen was the kind hidden in drawers in hotels. Now I had a Bible of my very own, a Bible just for teens, required for Bible class, which I went to every day after history. It had pink bubbles in between the actual Bible text, telling us how to use the Bible verses to behave, things about modesty and kindness. But the instructions were vague, and I still didn't know how to act in front of the other kids at school, if they could tell I was godless, what the rules actually were for Christians. I didn't know if you were allowed to like rap videos or curse. Rachel liked rap videos. She cursed.

When the video ended, Rachel muted the TV and picked up the phone. She had her own line, the same clear Conair phone I had in my own room. She told the person our order and her address, sounding just like a grown-up, like she ordered pizzas for herself all the time.

III.

We had chapel every day and I hated it. Everyone bowed their head and closed their eyes, and I just sat there, alone. Instead of praying I watched the other people. My favorite person to stare at was this girl Michelle, who was very good and never said anything mean. When she prayed, her face grew still, calm and serene like a princess in a Disney movie. One time the sun was coming through the window in a way that made it look like rays from heaven were shining down on her head, and she looked so peaceful and whole. That night I tried to pray to Jesus before I went to sleep but it didn't work. All I felt was crazy, like I was talking to the wall.

But now I had Rachel to sit next to. Rachel didn't bow her head or close her eyes either. Now we could keep our eyes open and our heads straight ahead, together. Now I had someone to laugh with whenever they talked about Jesus entering somebody, which happened a lot, Jesus, the sex pervert, always getting up in other people's bodies.

Mr. Bryson led the songs. He was the Bible teacher and he knew how to play guitar. He was a surfer and was always describing God's love as *gnarly* and *awesome*. He taught in NVC sweat-shorts every day, the kind we wore in PE, and he sat on the desk and tried to make us think the Bible was cool, and the sweat-shorts always bunched around his balls.

That day he was teaching us a new song. In the movies, people singing in church were always kind of beautiful: people singing about blood, people in robes singing like angels, people clapping their hands. In chapel, though, the songs were bland and stupid and there was not a single beautiful thing about them. In dull flat voices, we were made to sing about how God was an awesome God and some weird song about a deer.

The new song was worse than all the rest. It was a Monkees song that I think maybe Mr. Bryson made up to pretend it was about Jesus. He said *His face* instead of *her face*, with a big capital *H*, and then wham, suddenly it was a song not about romantic love but about worshipping our Lord and savior. *I'm a believer, in my redeemer, Jesus Christ.* I looked around at all the faces, all the kids around me, singing the song like it was fine, like it was normal, like it didn't suck out their soul and make them want to die. I wanted to leave, but whenever I'd tried to "go to the bathroom" during chapel, the teachers wouldn't let me.

I couldn't handle it so finally I just stood up. I started singing. I sang the terrible song in my terrible voice as loud as I could, flat and off-key. *Not a trace of doubt in my mind. I am loved. Now I'm a believer.*

Rachel giggled, stood up, began to sing loud with me. I started flapping my hands and rolling my eyes like I'd seen in the movies, people in tents, carried away by the spirit of the Lord. Rachel flapped her hands and rolled her eyes too. She jumped up and down. We were believers in our redeemer, Jesus Christ. I felt a lightness in my chest and in my feet and maybe it really was God, maybe God was just a feeling of happiness.

Mr. Wagner, the headmaster, came over to us with an angry look on his face.

"Girls," he said, "stop that right now."

"But Mr. Wagner," I said, "I'm filled with the spirit." I was trying so hard not to laugh. "I'm filled with the spirit of the Lord." I didn't look at Rachel. I couldn't. I was trying so hard to sound serious.

There was nothing he could say to that. You can't argue with a person when they're filled with the spirit of the Lord. He walked away. We kept singing. We kept flapping our hands. I didn't hate chapel that day.

IV.

We were in Latin class. I didn't know why they made us take Latin. They claimed it would make us better at French and Spanish but I didn't understand why we didn't just take French and Spanish instead. The Latin teacher was old and wore big thick glasses. His name was Mr. Bates. We called him Master Bates but only behind his back, because Mr. Bates was weird and old but nice. He pretended not to notice when we cheated on the tests, thumbing our textbooks to fill in the conjugation tables.

Rachel was across the room from me because we had assigned seats. I was trying to catch her eye. Mr. Bates was telling us the same old joke again, something about a boy with no limbs who rolled down a hill. The punch line was "Stop while you're a head." He said it in English, then in Latin. Rachel and I had just been talking about how weird the joke was before class, why he had this compulsion to constantly say it.

There was a blank look on her face. I watched her nail-bitten fingers grab a strand of hair from her head. She had a pixie cut, which she held back with plastic barrettes. The strand was just long enough for her to stare straight at it, right in front of her eyes. Then she twisted a single hair, yanked it out. She looked at it for a moment, stretched between her fingers, before laying it neatly on her desk. I watched her do it again—look at the hair, pull it out, look at it, place it on her desk—and again. One of the weirdest things I'd ever seen. I kept looking around to see if anyone else noticed. I didn't want to be known as the friend of the weird hair plucker.

I walked over to her the second the class ended. On her desk, there was a thin bundle of hair, lined up neatly like toothpicks.

Rachel was still sitting there, spaced out. I grabbed her arm.

"Come on," I said.

She jolted like she'd been asleep.

"What are you doing?" I whispered so no one would hear.

"I like looking at the root," she said. "See?" She held one hair in front of my eyes.

"It's a hair," I said.

"The end is a different color."

I didn't know what to say to that so I just left. I could hear her gathering her books as I walked through the door.

V.

My schedule had gotten messed up somehow, so I had PE with ninth graders. They all ignored me at first, with their tits and their makeup, but soon they found out I was good at sports.

Heather was good at sports too. She managed to look cool in her ratty PE outfit, rolling the waistband of her shorts and the sleeves of her shirt until they flattered her body, her legs long, pulled-up striped knee socks like the hot girls in *Dazed and Confused*. She was really pretty, a pointy chin and big wide eyes like a cat. She was team captain and she started picking me first for her teams, and then she started sitting next to me when we did stretches, talking to me in the locker room, offering to let me use her perfume. I don't know why she liked me. I was fast and I played hard, just like her, but that was the only good thing about me.

Usually we were only PE friends, talking during class but that was it. The high school was on one side of campus, the junior high on another, and there was no reason for us to see each other in between. But one day we left the locker room to go to lunch and she just stayed by my side instead of going to eat with her ninth-grade friends. I got a burrito at the stand and Heather waited in line with me. Then Rachel came out of class and found me. "Hey," she said, in the middle of Heather talking. Heather stopped, took her in, Rachel's bug eyes, stick legs, short hair.

"This is Rachel," I said. "Rachel, this is Heather."

"Hi," they said, and then Heather went back to what she was saying.

We got our burritos and sat on the bench by the front of the school. Rachel was weird and quiet the whole time. She didn't eat much of her burrito, instead ripping the tortilla into shreds. It was gross. When she was done, I saw her fingers go to her head, pick a strand. She caught herself, put her hands under her legs. Heather didn't notice.

VI.

Rachel was no longer the weirdest kid in class. That title now belonged to Dan Patterson, who wouldn't stop beating off under his desk. It was funny because he was always doing things to show what a good Christian he was, like raising money for the people whose homes had been destroyed in that year's fires. He always closed his eyes in chapel, squinching them shut and moving his mouth as he prayed. He got As on everything, which actually wasn't that big of a deal because I did too, but you wouldn't know that by the way he acted whenever we got a test back, holding out his paper so people could see the letter grade and smiling. I knew enough about the Bible by this point to know you weren't supposed to do that. In this way, I was a better Christian than him. When I got an A, I looked at my grade and then I put the paper in my binder, like a normal fucking person.

The first time I saw him do it, I thought it must have been a mistake, that maybe he was doing something normal, just jiggling his leg. His textbook was over his lap, and his hand was in his pocket, shaking the textbook back and forth. I was sitting only two seats away and it made me feel sick so I turned to look at the wall. I couldn't believe he was actually doing that, that he thought nobody would notice and the book over his lap was enough of a cover. I looked at him again, just to check. He was totally beating off.

He started to do it every day, and then every class. He

even did it while the teacher called on him. Everybody pretended not to notice, the other students, the teachers. They all said mean things about nonbelievers and gay people, yet according to them this was perfectly fine, an action so small it wasn't worth mentioning. Nobody said anything. They just ignored it. They always ignored everything that mattered.

VII.

It was Saturday. Rachel's mom dropped us off in La Jolla and gave her some money. I'd never been to downtown La Jolla to go shopping. My mom always took me to the mall. I thought downtown La Jolla was all stodgy rich people and rich-people clothing, and it was those things but there were a couple cool stores too. We went into a tiny store that had a girl with a nose ring at the cash register. All the clothes were cool brands I'd seen in magazines and on MTV but never before in real life. Everything was cute and expensive.

Rachel took a spaghetti-strap dress off the rack, held it up to her chest. "Oh," she said in a voice that wasn't hers. "Oh, it's just perfect. I could totally wear this to the pool when we're in Spain and then put on a sweater in the evening. Day to night. I must try it on."

I caught on quick. I grabbed a dress too, a baby doll in big flowers that cost $129. "I'm so glad my dad got us first-class tickets," I said. "Only losers fly coach."

We had a whole itinerary down by the time we got to the dressing room, arms filled with hundreds of dollars' worth of clothes, museums and restaurants and discotheques. The nose ring girl seemed happy to let us try them on.

We pretended none of the clothes fit right, which was a lie—some of them were so cute it hurt to not go home with them. The nose ring girl kept offering to help us, bringing us different dresses, different sizes. She seemed disappointed when Rachel only bought a pack of barrettes and I only bought a cheap necklace. At the cash register, there was a display of a new kind of nail polish, which came in colors like green and purple and black. They each had a plastic jewel ring on the handle and I wanted one so bad but I didn't have enough money. "Oh, and the playa," Rachel said. "Have you ever been to the playa?"

"Yeah, the last time I went to Spain." I didn't even know what a playa was. I pulled out my allowance money, and then I watched Rachel's hand slip over a bottle of pale purple polish. The nose ring girl hadn't noticed. Rachel tucked the bottle up her sleeve. The nose ring girl handed me my change. We left the store.

"I was trying to steal one of the tank tops," Rachel said. "But that bitch kept on bothering us." I'd never stolen anything before and was a little shocked and a little impressed, but I laughed and pretended it was no big deal.

We went across the street to the bakery and bought cookies and then we had no more money. There was still a half hour until Rachel's mom picked us up. We went down to the Church of Scientology and sat on the steps, painting our nails with the purple polish in the sun. When Rachel's mom finally got us, the nail polish had just dried.

VIII.

Mrs. Norman, the PE teacher, took Heather and me aside and said we couldn't be on the same team anymore. I was now the other team captain. It was the soccer portion of the school year, the sport that Heather and I were best at, the kicking and the running. Athletics were a God-given gift and it simply wasn't fair to have the two most talented athletes on the same team, she said. We had to spread the talent around.

At first it was fine. Heather's team won on Monday. On Tuesday, we tied. I won on Wednesday. We were spreading the talent around. But then I won on Thursday, and Friday too.

The following Monday, my team was winning again. Heather's face was different as we played, and her tilty cat eyes looked at me like she hated me, like I was the worst and most disgusting thing in the world. I had the ball and was dribbling it down the field and she was trying to take it from me but she couldn't. Suddenly she slammed me with her shoulder. I stumbled a little and she got the ball. We weren't supposed to do that, to check each other, but Mrs. Norman hadn't noticed. I got so mad that I couldn't see for a minute, the anger bursting black spots in front of my eyes. I ran toward her. And then without thinking, I was kicking her, hard, in the shin, with my new cleats. Heather fell. I got the ball. I kicked it straight into the center of the goal from the halfway line, a perfect shot. But it didn't matter. Mrs.

Norman was blowing her whistle and then she was standing next to Heather. Neither one of them had seen my goal.

I walked over to them. Heather was sitting on the grass on her butt, blood streaming from her shin, staining her white socks. I'd caught her cleanly on the bone with my cleats. The other girls were already gathered around her.

"You psycho!" she screamed at me.

I was breathing heavy and my head still felt hot. I swallowed the urge to kick her again, apologized instead, but Heather didn't want to hear. It was an accident, I lied. We should probably wear shin guards, I said. Nobody was listening to me.

Mrs. Norman cleaned the cut, applied a Band-Aid, and made the two of us sit on the benches for the rest of the period. I could feel Heather's anger pulsing off her as she sat there silently, refusing to look in my direction. I didn't care. My anger pulsed right back at her, stronger and harder. I replayed the look on her face as she had sat on the ground, bleeding. I smiled.

IX.

Going over to Rachel's mom's meant that a lot of the time
she took us to the Beach and Tennis Club, where she had
a membership. Her mom would get her nails or hair done
at the salon, or she'd just drop us off, a place to dump us.
Usually we got cheeseburgers at the café and charged them
to her account.

We went there almost every day during Spring Break.
We'd been trying to become smokers for a while but it was
hard to get cigarettes. None of our parents smoked. That
day we ordered cheeseburgers and ate them and then we
were bored. We got the idea to go around to the ashtrays
and find some cigarettes that weren't smoked down that
much. It took a while but eventually we found an old Marlboro and an old Camel, barely smoked. Rachel took some
matches from the stand at the restaurant and we went into
the bushes by the duck pond to smoke them.

"Is this gross?" I said.

"What?"

"Smoking other people's cigarettes. Like what if this
Marlboro person had herpes."

"Oh well," Rachel said. "Guess I'll get herpes."

The cigarette smoke tasted gross but by the third puff I
was starting to like it. I had to think to inhale, remind myself to let the smoke get in my lungs rather than just sitting
in my mouth.

Some ducks were by the water, plain and brown. I watched them peck their flat bills in the dirt. I took another drag, watched a boy duck walk up, its neck a dazzling jade.

"Why do we call that a boy duck and not a man duck?" I said.

"Is that a joke?" Rachel said.

"No, it's just weird. You call it a male duck or a boy duck and that," I said, pointing to the brown ducks, "you call a female duck or a girl duck, but if you called them women and men, that'd be weird."

"Look at that MAN duck," Rachel said in a deep voice. "He's so MANLY. I wonder if he wants to go watch some SPORTS."

I laughed. I watched the man duck walk fast up to a woman duck. The woman duck turned her head around and made a *beep-beep* noise like a car. And then the man duck was on top of the woman duck, acting like a scary man and raping her. She was squawking.

"Ahhhhhh," I said, and ran toward the ducks like a toddler.

The man duck didn't want to get off, but then I got closer and it finally did.

Its duck dick was sticking out. It was bright red and looked like a fat squiggly piece of pasta.

"Oh my god," Rachel said. "Is that its dick?"

"Oh my god," I said. "Why does it look like pasta."

"That's so fucking gross."

"Rachel," I heard someone yell.

It was Rachel's mom. She was looking for us. "Shit," Rachel said. "We smell like smoke."

"Shit," I said.

"Do you have anything?" I said.

She had some cucumber body spray in her purse and we sprayed ourselves and got out of the bushes. I didn't know if we still smelled but Rachel's mom didn't say anything in the car. She never really said anything though, ever.

X.

Rachel and I were lab partners in science class. One of us was supposed to add ingredients to test tubes and the other was supposed to record the reactions, but I was doing all the work. Rachel was just sitting on the stool, staring out the window and pulling out her hair. The hair pulling had gotten bad over break. There was a big bald spot in the front that looked pink and raw and shiny. I had noticed it a few days ago, when she spent the night at my house. She now wore fat headbands and bandanas every day to cover it, anchored in place with bobby pins so they wouldn't move. I kept waiting for somebody to notice, to say something, to ask why she suddenly had big things on her head all the time, but nobody did. It was embarrassing. I still liked Rachel but I wanted her to be normal.

"Can you do some work?" I asked her. "Like add this to the beaker?"

Rachel looked at me but said nothing.

"Stop picking your hair and fucking help me," I whispered.

Her cheeks turned a bit pink and I knew I'd embarrassed her but I didn't care. "Put this in the beaker," I said.

She was supposed to carefully measure a scoop but instead she just shoved the spoon in the baggie and dumped it in. The liquid fizzed all over, onto the table and our worksheet. I pulled the paper off the desk, trying to not ruin my work, but then I remembered the experiment was about acids and bases and I didn't want to burn my hand off so I dropped it on the floor.

"Girls," Mrs. Green said. "What happened here?"

"It spilled," I said. Rachel just stood there, saying nothing.

Mrs. Green went into the cabinet, got us long gloves and things to clean up the mess. She seemed annoyed.

"Help me," I said to Rachel.

Rachel took a paper towel from the roll and dabbed it at the desk. Then she took off the gloves, got back on her stool while I cleaned up the rest. I caught her not plucking her hair but doing something new. She was ripping out her eyelashes. She didn't do it neatly like the hair. Instead it was just *rip* and then she threw the lash on the floor.

It took a while to clean up the mess by myself. We didn't finish the worksheet. At the end of the period, Mrs. Green picked it up by the corner and it was wet and incomplete. She threw it away and told us we got a C. I had perfect As in that class and now stupid Rachel had ruined everything.

I had a pencil in my hand. I made a fist around it, so tight that it snapped in half. I felt the sharp pain of a splinter lodging in my thumb. I threw the pencil shards in the trash. I didn't talk to Rachel for the rest of the day. I ate my lunch alone, working the splinter out with my teeth.

XI.

Right before the end of the school year, we all went for three days on a spiritual retreat. That's what they called it. It was an hour away in Ramona. The girls stayed in one wing in bunk beds, the boys in another. All day we did normal camp things, hikes and crafts and meals in a cafeteria, and at night we had chapel, Mr. Bryson leading us in the same old terrible songs.

Except the last night we had a real pastor. I don't know where they got him from, but he was tall and handsome like a Ken doll, wearing a crisp denim shirt and black slacks. He led us in prayer and then told us some Bible stories, this one about somebody who was willing to sacrifice his son, which seemed fucked-up, his voice louder and clearer and more confident than Mr. Bryson's. Before he'd been mellow and smiled a lot, but now he had on a Serious Face. He started to tell us about hell. He was telling us that if we didn't live the right way, we would suffer until the end of time. He told us what hell was like, how it was so hot and it smelled like sulfur, and all you heard were screams, and all you saw were people in pain, rolling their eyes and gnashing their teeth and pulling at their hair.

After he'd gone on about hell for what seemed like for-ever, detailing every little thing we'd see and hear, every sin that could put us there, he changed gears. He'd been talking in a loud, urgent voice, but somehow it became louder and more urgent, his eyes bugging out of his head, sweat rings appearing under his armpits, like he was high. He wanted us to know we could be saved, that we didn't have to burn in hell, that all we had to do was Ask Jesus Into Our Heart. He repeated that phrase a whole bunch, talking about how great it was, how we'd never be alone, how our hearts would always be filled with warmth and our decisions would be guided by a quiet certainty. The way he talked, it was like Christianity was a secret club that magically solved everything.

He ended the whole rant by waving his arms around and saying, "Who wants to change their life tonight? Who wants to go to the Kingdom of Heaven and spend all of eternity cradled in the Good Lord's hand? Which of you is truly on fire for the Lord? Come forth."

When he finally stopped speaking, the whole chapel was so quiet and still. It seemed like he was waiting for us to do something, but I wasn't sure what, maybe raise our hands or yell, "Me! I'm on fire!"

But then I saw Michelle, the perfect Christian, walk up to the stage.

"Come forth, child!" the pastor yelled at her. "Come forth and cast your sins!"

She stood onstage like she was accepting a prize, her posture perfectly straight, eyes bright and shiny, her blond hair gleaming under the lights. "Bless you, child," the pastor said, and hugged her. He made her get down on her knees, and told her to ask Him into her heart. He touched her on the forehead as she knelt.

Michelle sat there quietly while we all stared, and it was like she was the only person in the room, her eyes closed, her lips moving, asking Jesus to enter her. Nobody laughed. When she stood up she was crying. Jesus was inside her.

"Can you feel it?" the pastor said. "Can you feel the strength of Jesus? Who else will come up here and repent?"

Dan Patterson stood up. He was already crying as he walked, probably feeling bad about all the masturbation. He knelt down and the pastor touched him on the head, and then a couple other nerdy kids went up, and they repented and asked Jesus to enter them too, and they cried, and the pastor yelled more about could we feel it, and then suddenly there was a line to be saved, not just nerdy kids anymore, but everyone, and they were all crying, and the emotion was so high that it felt like the whole room was vibrating. Everyone was crying and asking Jesus into their heart. Everyone was on fire for the Lord. And soon there were so many of my classmates up there that they couldn't all fit onstage, so then they began to kneel in front of it, and everyone seemed to know what to do, seemed to know the important thing was getting up there and kneeling and whispering until the pastor came over and touched their heads, and then it was time for them to stand up and cry. Tears streaming down people's faces, and no one was the least bit ashamed of it. They were proud. And everyone was hugging and crying.

The pastor walked around, repeating the same phrases: *Bless you, child. You have been saved. Ask Jesus into your heart. Repent.*

I went to turn to Rachel and whisper about how creepy this whole fucking thing was, and she wasn't there. I looked around and I saw her waiting in line. I studied her face to see if she was crying. It didn't look like she was. She kneeled, curled over herself like everyone else was doing. She was very still. She sat there for a while, her head lowered so I couldn't tell if she was whispering and crying or just sitting there. Finally the pastor touched her head, saying "Bless you, child," and she stood, slowly, as though waking from a long nap. Her face was still and calm, and she looked peaceful, and I could see a ring of light around her, her face lit on fire by the Lord.

She looked so different, and I wanted to be different too. But I couldn't do it. I sat there, motionless. Dirty, unsaved, ready to burn in hell.

XII.

We were at the Beach and Tennis Club again. Rachel's mom had dropped us off and then went somewhere to meet her new boyfriend. We actually went to the beach that day, putting our swimsuits on in the locker room, which I hadn't been in before. The locker room didn't feel like it was infested with athlete's foot like the one at school or the one I'd been to when I was a kid, signed up for swimming lessons at the YMCA. This one was gleaming tile and fluffy towels. There was a hair dryer attached to the wall and a basket with little bottles of toiletries you could take. I grabbed a bottle of lotion and a bottle of hair spray and put them in my bag. I expected Rachel to take some but she said she had a bunch at home already. She looked in the mirror, checked her bandana, made sure the bobby pins were secure.

We grabbed some of the striped beach towels and took them down to the sand. It was hot that day, the light white and gleaming. We lay on the towels and I immediately felt sleepy and miserable. I hated the beach. I hated the sand. I hated wearing a bathing suit in public. The sun was too bright in my eyes and I wanted to flip over, but then my butt would be just there in the air. I closed my eyes and the world was red behind my eyelids.

"Brian," I heard Rachel yelling.

I opened my eyes. I saw two figures down the sand. They came over to us. It was two boys I'd never seen before, our age, scrawny and tan in board shorts. They'd known Rachel at Westlake Prep, the secular private school Rachel had gone to before NVC. My parents were going to send me there until they found out the tuition cost three times as much. They sat down beside us.

I wanted them to go away but they all blabbed about people I didn't know. I wrapped my towel around me, covering my belly and my flat chest. Rachel noticed.

"Are you covering your burning bush?" she asked.

"What?" I said.

"Your pubic hair. On your thighs."

I didn't know what she was talking about. I didn't know if I had pubic hair on my thighs, but I probably didn't because I only had about fifteen hairs to begin with. I felt myself flush red and I wanted to rip the bandana off Rachel's head but that seemed too mean, and I wanted to get up and walk away but I felt too self-conscious to do it wrapped in my towel and I felt too self-conscious to do it without being wrapped in my towel, so I just sat there staring at the sand, embarrassed and mad.

The boys went away a few minutes later. "Bye!" Rachel yelled in an annoying high voice.

"Why'd you say that?" I asked her. Now that the embarrassment was gone, I felt an anger twisting in my throat.

Rachel laughed uncomfortably. "I was just kidding," she said.

"It wasn't funny."

"Okay, jeez, sorry," she said. "Let's go swimming."

I agreed, put my hair up in a bun so it wouldn't get wet and frizzy.

We sat down in the water, before the wave break, where it was warm and shallow. I felt the water rise and fall on my thighs and the sand crabs wiggled under my butt, leaving trails beside me in the wet sand. I dug my hand into the sand and caught a couple of them in my palm, the way I had when we first moved to San Diego and I went to the beach every day, when the water and the sand were still a novelty.

"Gross," Rachel said about the sand crabs. I pinched one between my fingers, let its tiny legs crawl in the air, put it back in the sand, watched it vanish.

Rachel was suddenly splashing me, her hands twirling in the water.

"Cut it out," I said. "I don't want to get my hair wet."

But she just aimed higher, the salt water getting in my eyes, stinging. And it all boiled over, everything that frustrated me about Rachel, her comment about the pubic hair, the way she always stared off into space, her bald head. I wasn't thinking about what I was doing but suddenly I was on top of her, straddling her. I punched her in the stomach and she went down in the water. I pinned her shoulders with my hands. I could see her eyes bugging out under the water and I just wanted her to stop moving. Her arms were trying to thrash around but I was too strong and she couldn't really move. I held her down under the water for a moment longer and then I let her up.

She was sputtering, eyes red, a trail of yellow snot from her nose. The bandana had fallen off her head and was lying wet in the water. Her bald spot gleamed white in the sun.

DUST PARTICLES

Mom took the divorce money and moved us to a condo the summer before third grade. There were hardly any kids in the complex and school hadn't started yet, so I didn't have anyone to play with. It was looking like a boring summer. She wouldn't let me go to the pool or the playground or anywhere fun alone.

But a couple weeks in, there was a girl at the pool. She was exactly my age and real little with red hair. Her name was Katie. She taught me to do handstands at the bottom of the pool, and later I showed her how to bake cookies. We both liked Ninja Turtles over Barbies and knew how to ride our bikes without training wheels. We decided to become best friends.

Then one day after we'd just gotten back from the pool, Katie told me we were going to play girlfriend and boyfriend. I didn't know what that meant and she said I'd find out. She said it in a way that made it seem like it would be exciting. Then she told me to get on the bed.

All of a sudden she was on top of me. I didn't know what she was doing.

"I'm your boyfriend," she said in a growly voice, "and you like this."

She put her mouth over mine before I could say anything and stuck her tongue in. She pointed it around my mouth, swirling in circles. My teeth felt cold. Her eyes were closed like they did on TV but I left mine open so I could watch her. It looked like she was an alien and she was eating off my face. Her hair was still wet and it tickled my shoulders.

"Okay," she said after a bit. "It's time to have sex now."

I didn't really understand how sex worked yet because I wasn't allowed to watch rated-R movies. I thought you needed a man and a woman to do it, but I wasn't sure and I didn't want to look dumb.

We took off our clothes and stood there in silence for a moment. The lights were off and the blinds were closed. One of the slats toward the bottom had broken, and the sun shone through the gap, the beam ending next to my foot. I watched the dust dance around. Last year in school, I'd learned that dust was mostly particles of skin and each month we breathed in three grams of dust. The two facts together meant we were always breathing in people. I looked at Katie's naked body and told myself that the skin I was looking at would be dust someday. I looked at her naked body and told myself I was already breathing her in.

"Get back on the bed," she told me.

"How are we supposed to have sex?" I asked.

She looked at me like I was very stupid. "We rub our privates together," she said. "How do you not know that?"

I really didn't want to play this game anymore but it seemed like it was too late to stop. I got back on the bed and closed my eyes. I wanted to pretend that I was asleep, or maybe not even asleep but dead. I made my whole body limp. Katie crawled on top of me and moved around until one of her legs was between mine and vice versa. She started thrusting at me and making grunting sounds and something warm and strange started happening between my legs. I wanted to jump up but sleeping people don't move, so I tried to stay there and I tried to stay still. But I couldn't. I couldn't keep playing the game. I pushed her away and flew off the bed. My bathing suit was on the floor and I picked it up and ran into the bathroom and locked the door. I got dressed and then I stared at myself in the mirror for a long time, until my eyes became just eyes and my mouth no longer looked like my own.

When I got out, I expected Katie to be dressed but she wasn't. She was still sitting on the bed. "You kicked me in the stomach," she said, "when you pushed me off of you."

"I have to go home," I said, and then I went. I didn't look at her as I left the room and I didn't say goodbye.

I decided I probably shouldn't play with her for a while but I didn't hold out very long. It was my mom's fault, I guess. She came into the room one day and I was just lying there on the carpet biting my cuticles. It was one of my bad habits. I don't know how long I'd been there, but it was long enough that they'd started to bleed. "Good god," my mom said. "Go outside and play or something. Go play with Katie."

I was so bored that I'd kind of forgotten why I'd decided I didn't want to play with Katie in the first place. I stopped biting my cuticles and went to her house. We played Little House on the Prairie and I got to be Laura. Afterward, her mom made us quesadillas.

A couple weeks went by and school started. Katie was in a different class, but I still played with her more than anybody else because she lived so close. When my birthday came, Katie gave me one of those necklaces that is a jagged half of a heart. Mine said BEST and hers said FRIENDS. I'd always wanted one of those, had wondered when I'd get one, and now here it was. But in my head, I'd imagined the necklace as silver like the moon, and the necklace Katie gave me was glittery plastic. In my head, the best friend and I could talk to each other with looks because we knew the thoughts in each other's heads so well. In real life, sometimes I would catch Katie staring off into space, completely unaware of anything going on around her, and I had no idea where she was in her mind or what she was thinking.

I went to her house one day near Halloween. We were supposed to work on our costumes. Katie's mom had a big sewing machine and she was going to help. We had just seen *The Wizard of Oz*. Katie wanted to be the Tin Man, but a Tin Girl, and I wanted to be the Wicked Witch.

Her dad answered the door. He was hardly ever home. He never smiled. "Linda's at the store, I think," he said. Linda was Katie's mom. I never called her Linda, though. I never called her anything. It felt weird for her to be called that. "I don't know when she'll be back. Katie's upstairs in her room."

I walked upstairs, disappointed. I wanted a scary witch dress and funny witch stockings and now I wasn't sure if I'd get them at all. I pictured my mom and me going to CVS, looking for a witch costume, one of the store-bought ones that's itchy and doesn't fit right, except all that was left were some Power Rangers and a ninja. No Wicked Witch for me.

When I got upstairs I saw Katie standing in her doorway, waiting. She wasn't wearing anything except for big gold sunglasses I guess she'd stolen from her dad. Her hand was on her hip. "There's my little girl," she said in a weird voice. It was like she was acting something out of a movie.

My heart started pounding. It felt like something very bad was happening.

"Katie," her dad's voice came from behind me. I guess he'd followed me up the stairs and I hadn't noticed. He was talking in a quiet voice, but even though it was quiet I still felt afraid. "What are you doing?" he asked her. He seemed mad, mad in a way like this was something they had already talked about.

She hadn't moved, wasn't even trying to cover herself. Her hand was still on her hip, freckles interrupting the whiteness of her skin. "It's so hot," she said. "I was hot."

It wasn't hot in the house. I was so embarrassed even though I wasn't doing anything wrong. Except her father was staring at me like I was. It was like he was trying to figure out what I was thinking, trying to figure out what he should do to me, how I deserved to be punished. I didn't know where I was supposed to look or what I should say so I kept quiet and stared at my shoes but I could feel my cheeks burning like they were on fire.

"Put your dress on," he said finally.

I heard shuffling, Katie getting dressed, but I refused to look away from the ground. I didn't want to be the Wicked Witch anymore. I wanted to be anything else, anything at all, anything that wasn't made by Katie's mom and anything that wasn't wicked. I'd be a Power Ranger. I'd love wearing my itchy costume. I'd love wearing my pink plastic mask.

I looked up again when the shuffling stopped. Katie was wearing clothes now, but the two of them were standing in the same spots as before: Katie in the doorway, with her hand on her hip, her father across from her, both of them looking at each other in a way that made me feel like things that didn't need words were being said between them.

I looked down at the floor again. I wanted to be safe. The carpet upstairs was fluffy and dark blue. I remembered how one day, when I'd first met Katie, back before anything bad had happened, her mother had gotten a new microwave. We took the box upstairs and pretended it was a ship and the carpet was a sea and we were sailors.

The carpet had fresh vacuum lines in it, but there was a thin strip running right below the wall that was dusty and gray, where the vacuum couldn't reach. The dusty strip was dust. The dusty strip was also pieces of people. There was some of my skin in there, mixed with Katie's skin, mixed with her dad's skin, mixed with Linda's. Even if I left right now and never came back, some of me would stay right there in that carpet. Some of them would be in my lungs, and some of me would be floating in that air, waiting to be sucked in.

THE RYANS

We waited all evening for Naomi's parents to leave, a cord of excitement running taut between the two of us. When their Land Rover finally pulled out of the driveway, we waited ten extra minutes, just in case they forgot something and came back. Only then did we take the rolled-up scarf from Naomi's closet, a neat package containing a lighter and two perfectly rolled joints, the result of Naomi practicing with tobacco while me and my clumsy fingers sat and watched. We crawled out her bedroom window onto the roof.

We pressed ourselves against the wall in case her neighbors could see, lit the first joint. The days were finally starting to get longer, and even though it was almost eight, there were still traces of light in the air, the sky that cobalt blue right before it turns black. We held the smoke in, the way we'd seen people do in movies. It made us cough. It made us feel cool.

We'd gotten the weed from the Ryans, the only other friends we had at the Christian school. Except *friends* wasn't entirely accurate. The less cute Ryan, Ryan M., lived down the street from Naomi, so the three of us carpooled each morning. Ryan D. was Ryan M.'s best friend. We sat together at lunch, occasionally hung out voluntarily after school and on weekends. We liked the same music and swapped mixtapes. We smoked. We got sent out of class for talking, sometimes stayed in at lunch for detention.

That was the friend part. But the Ryans could be mean. They liked to call us "flat-tittied bitches." They made fun of my acne and Naomi's thick thighs. They asked us if we liked nonexistent bands, and if we said we weren't sure but thought we did they called us posers. I tried to brush it off—maybe they saw us as their little sisters—but in truth they made me cry. I never admitted it, not to Naomi, not to anyone, but it was hard to go into the bathroom and be confronted with the smattering of red bumps on my forehead that wouldn't go away and not hear their nasty voices telling me I was disgusting, saying things like "Hey, pimple girl," the way they did when my skin was especially bad. It made me envision stabbing my pencil into their eyes, blood running squishy, and their screams.

Also, they were always going on about all the weed they smoked. But I never saw them do it, never saw them stoned either. I'd never smoked pot before, but I wanted to. Same with Naomi. But we had no idea where to get it. Partially we didn't ask them to get us some because I wasn't sure the Ryans were telling the truth, but mostly I was afraid they'd make fun of us.

One day we were sitting around Ryan M.'s room after school, playing video games because we had nothing better to do, and once again they wouldn't shut up about how they'd gotten so high that weekend, drawing out the vowels the way the skateboarders did in the skate videos we sometimes watched. Finally I got to the point where I couldn't stand it anymore so I just came right out and asked where they got it.

They were quiet for a moment, and I thought they were trying to think of some sick burns. But then Ryan D. said, "None of your business," at the same time Ryan M. said, "From my brother."

Then they called us dumb little babies for never having smoked pot.

"Fuck you," Naomi said.

"Yeah," I said. "Fuck you." I was so sick of their shit, of them acting like they were so much better than us when they were two stupid junior high boys, with no facial hair and skinny chests. "You're fucking lying anyway."

"Whoa, somebody's on their period," Ryan M. said, and I rolled my eyes at him, his stupid insults not even original or funny.

"Let's bounce," Naomi said.

"Good idea."

So we left. We went back to her house and watched TV.

The next day at school, they acted like nothing had happened. At lunch, they came and sat with us and were nice, asking us what we were doing that weekend and did we want to record Ryan D.'s new Descendents album. Naomi and I just looked at them. Yesterday we had agreed we were sick of them. This niceness was fucking everything up. And then

Ryan M. said if we really wanted pot, he could get us some from his brother. We pretended it wasn't a big deal, that we didn't care either way, but I could tell by the look in Naomi's eyes and the flutter in my chest that we were excited.

After we smoked the joints, we felt nothing. We waited half an hour just in case, then took the rest of the "weed" and compared it to the herb jars in the kitchen. Just as we thought. It was oregano.

We should have known the weed was bunk when they didn't try to smoke it with us. We should have known the weed was bunk when Ryan D. said that sometimes you had to smoke weed a couple times before you got high. But we didn't know any better, had no idea what weed was supposed to look like other than a dried green plant, which is what they sold us.

So we made a plan. On Wednesdays, Ryan M. didn't carpool home because he had tutoring. His older brother had baseball practice every day. His mother didn't get home until at least four. We didn't know his dad's work schedule but we figured it was a dad work schedule, and he wouldn't be home until five or six.

We told Naomi's mom we were going to buy ice cream. The door to Ryan M.'s garage was unlocked, just like usual, tools perfectly lined up on the wall on their hooks. From there we walked into the house, and then up the stairs to his room. I kept thinking someone would catch us, his brother home sick or the cleaning lady, but then I remembered what dickheads they were, the twenty dollars they'd stolen from us, and I told myself the house was empty and it was fine and he deserved everything we'd planned.

We opened the door to his room. There was underwear on the floor, dingy white boxers, and the bed was unmade, but otherwise it looked the same as it always did. Posters on the wall of hot chicks and Kelly Slater. A wall of CDs, a big TV, a big stereo.

We'd bought a can of sardines a few days earlier at the grocery store. I popped it open, the metal lid flicking the nasty oil onto my hand. We put the fish where we figured he wouldn't look, grabbing them by their slimy tails. In the heating vent on the floor. Underneath the bed. I went into his closet, and Naomi boosted me up while I hid one on the top shelf, behind a plastic bin of baseball cards. His bookshelf only held old schoolbooks—a Latin dictionary, the textbook from Pre-algebra 1, *To Kill a Mockingbird*—so I pulled them out half an inch and tucked one behind. We put two behind his stereo.

Naomi went to put one in his desk drawer, but when she slid it open, she found a big rusty hunting knife. "Nice," I said. "I'm gonna take it."

"I found it," Naomi said. "You already have a knife." Mine was a tiny pocketknife that I kept in my purse, completely useless unless you wanted to open a box or whittle. This one was big and scary.

We stood there, trying to figure out who got to have it. But I started thinking about Ryan M.'s stupid face, his cocky smile, the fact that he seemed completely unaware he was an idiot with dirty boxers on his floor. And I took the knife and stabbed it into the desk, which looked expensive, pretending I was stabbing him. Stab stab stab. It felt so good. I imagined his screams.

Naomi laughed. The knife made neat little gashes, splitting the thick waxed coating of the desk. She took it from my hand, stabbed again. The wood splintered this time. Then I stabbed it, a whole bunch of times, hard, like I was trying to kill it. Like I was trying to get deep at the bones. Naomi did the same, yelping this time like a warrior. I was laughing. She was laughing. We were two maniacal bitches, and the Ryans would be sorry they fucked with us. I took the knife and stabbed it in the desk one final time, deep enough that it stood up straight on its own. Then we changed his radio from the rock station to a Spanish one, turned the volume up, so loud the bass crackled in the speakers, and then turned it off so the next time he went to play it, it would scare the shit out of him.

We left his house, skipping and laughing our way back to Naomi's, throwing the empty can of sardines in the gutter. My heart beat fast in a way that wasn't fear. It was the heartbeat of a maniacal bitch. I kept imagining Ryan M.'s face when he walked in and saw the knife, when he turned on the stereo, when the fish started to rot.

I hoped it made him afraid.

I hoped it made him feel small.

ROADKILL

I killed a cat before I left. I was supposed to go home real quick, get out of my work clothes, grab my bag. The sun was at a bad angle, slicing through the dirty windshield into my eyes, and I didn't see the cat until it was too late.

The cat didn't look too bad, lying there like it could just be sleeping—except for its right eye, which was pooling in blood. It breathed in and out, loud and jagged. I stood over it. It didn't lift its head or even look at me.

A Jeep drove past as I was standing there, two girls a few years younger than me. They probably went to my old high school, the one I'd dropped out of a year before, long blond hair and light tans, bikinis tied in knots around their necks. The Jeep was brand-new, shiny white, pink and yellow daisies appliquéd to the back.

They pulled over. "Fuck," I said. They were going to come over here and make me feel bad about the cat.

"*Oh my god,*" one of the girls yelled.

"*Oh my god,*" the other girl yelled.

I thought for a second that the cat was theirs. The one in the cutoffs felt around its neck for a collar. The cat was still doing the jagged breathing.

"*What did you do?????*" the one in the miniskirt yelled at me. She was slightly less attractive than the other one, bigger nose, smaller chin.

"It ran in front of my car," I said. I tried to sound sad. I felt horrible, this sucking feeling in my gut and shaky hands. "The sun was in my eyes. I couldn't see shit." I was about to tell them I wasn't speeding or anything and it wasn't my fault, but it was clear they didn't care.

"*Oh my god*," one of them yelled again.

"We have to take it to the vet," the other said.

It was after five and the vet around the corner was closed. Blood was spilling out of the cat's eye onto the pavement.

The girls cradled the cat—one at the legs, the other the head—like a heavy, sacred object. They carted it over to the back of the Jeep, not seeming to care if they stained their cute clothes with its blood. They drove off without saying anything to me.

There was blood on the pavement, just a little bit, a splotch the size of a lima bean. I had an urge to touch it but I didn't want to touch it, so I got back in my car. There was nothing else to do. I drove home. I changed. I got on the train.

I had a flask of cheap vodka, and my silver pill case was full. I couldn't stop thinking about the bloody eye. I shut my eyes and it was still there, red and wet. I bought a bottle of orange juice at the snack bar, drank the vodka, ate two pills. The setting sun skimmed off the ocean, a bright orange globe behind my eyelids. I felt like shit. I fell asleep.

The purpose of the trip was to party. We went to Santa Barbara as often as we could, to visit Krista and Abby and their studio apartment. I came on the train from San Diego, where we'd all grown up, and Blair and Cara drove from college in Santa Cruz.

In San Diego, I worked at the wine store and took a class online at the community college. Sometimes in the mornings I could barely get out of bed, this feeling like some beast was crouched on my chest. In Santa Barbara, I drank more but not alone, and I barely slept. I didn't know it until years later but it was a bad time for the rest of them too. Blair had been raped at college and Cara was close to getting kicked out of school. Abby's dad had just died and Krista's Mormon family had cut her off.

It was like we were playing a game each weekend. We tried to outdo each other, and ourselves from the weekend before. There was the time we went to the porn party—they did a news story about it and we saw our dumb drunk faces on TV. There was the time we wore wet underwear in a kiddie pool, holding a sign asking for money for our abortions. Between all of it, half of us had spent a night in jail, less serious than it sounded. The cops took you away in a van, fed you a sandwich, and let you out in the morning.

Then there was the game we played out on Del Playa, the main street, which was crowded each weekend with thousands of students, thousands of strangers walking from party to party. We got a point for each penis we grabbed as we walked. The reactions varied. Sometimes the boys yelled and asked for our numbers. But most of them—we did it for the look on their faces. Pinched, flushing red, surprised. Afraid.

I didn't say anything about the cat when I got there. I was still thinking about it. I wanted it to go away. We shotgunned beers and I tried to push it out of my brain. A few beers in and it grew softer. I pretended it was something I saw in a movie. It floated out and away.

The girls wanted to go to the party at the big house next door. I didn't like those boys because they were stupid and boring. But I agreed to go anyway, didn't even complain. When we walked over, there was nobody there yet and the boys were playing pool. They offered us cups of punch, which we took, and then they ignored us. We sat on the couch and made up a new game.

We came up with the concept, the name, the rules. A "forority," an equal opportunity Greek fraternal organization, Delta Iota Kappa. If boys wanted to join, they had to show us their dicks. I took out the notebook I kept in my purse and we wrote all of it down.

Only one of the boys in the house was cute. His name was Remy. He was stupid and dressed bad but he looked like some guy in an underwear ad, blond hair and chiseled everything. Bright blue eyes. We called him over to us. We told him we needed a cute boy in our fororiry. "Just show us your dick," Cara said.

"It'll take one second," Blair said.

"Just a peek," I said.

"You'll get a patch," Abby said. "Sew it on your jacket."

Remy laughed. "You guys are crazy," he said. He seemed uncomfortable. Which was the point. He walked away.

Toward midnight we were sitting on the patio. I'd bought this jug of juice from the store because I thought the name was funny. Beefamato. It was Clamato but with beef broth instead of clam juice. We were trying to sell it to this boy. He was younger, only seventeen, had come up to visit his brother for the weekend. We told him it was mixed with vodka.

"Just try a sip," I said. "It's so strong."

He took a sip. Beef broth.

"Isn't it good?" Krista asked him.

"Oh man," I said. "I got so fucked-up from it last weekend."

"I don't taste anything," the boy said. "This shit is gross."

"It's the tomato juice," Cara said. "Haven't you ever had a Bloody Mary? You can't even taste the vodka."

"Oh yeah." He'd never had a Bloody Mary. "Okay," he said. "How much?"

"Twenty bucks," I said. "I paid forty."

"Why don't you want it?" he said.

"Last weekend was too much," I said.

"Oh my god, we got so fucked-up," Abby said.

"Just the thought of it makes me want to vomit," Blair said.

He gave us the twenty dollars. I put it in my pocket and we hopped over the patio wall. When we got in the alley we started laughing and couldn't stop. What an idiot.

At the store, we decided on whiskey. I liked the taste but forgot how it always made me mean. We drank it straight like shots, right in the alley. I had that heavy feeling in my feet but the rest of my body felt floaty and nice. The dead cat was long gone and I could do anything.

The bottle was just about empty when Remy came by. He was buying more beer for the party, he told us. The alley went from the apartment complex to the back entrance of the store. We were standing in the narrow part, a wooden fence and only enough room for one person. There was a hole in the fence, some planks removed, which was how you got to the store. Krista stood in front of the hole. I was near the fence, blocking the light from the patio, darkening everything except Remy's beautiful face in shadows.

"You're going to join our fororiety," Blair said.

"You have to," Krista said.

"Haha," Remy said. Something ran across his face like a rat. Fear.

I pushed him against the fence, a hand on each shoulder, hard. He seemed too startled to move.

"Get him," Cara said.

Krista grabbed his belt, tugged at it, released. I kept him pinned to the wood. His pants were at his ankles.

"Oh hey, hey," he said. He tried to bend down to pick up his pants, but I held on to his shoulders and he didn't fight back.

Blair reached through the hole in his boxers, found his cock.

"It's hard," she said. We laughed. It wasn't, but it was getting there. She tugged at it some, rough. I took one hand off his shoulder and cupped his balls.

Abby spat in her hand. She started jerking him off, sliding over the turkey neck to the tip. He still looked a little scared but was breathing heavy and it got heavier. Blair kissed him on the neck. I released his shoulders, took over for Abby. Cara grabbed his wrists and held them together. He was making little moans by then, jagged breaths, like the cat.

Blair stopped kissing him, got on her knees.

"Come on my tits," she said. She was wearing a T-shirt, so this was technically impossible. "Oh yeah, baby," she said, like a girl in a porno. "Come on my tits. Look at that cock. It's so hard. You're so hot, baby."

Remy's breathing got heavier. He made a soft cooing sound, like a baby. His face scrunched up. He came. Blair reached up, caught it in her hand. She stood, wiped it on his shirt. We laughed. Remy looked at the ground.

"You're fucking disgusting," Blair said.

"So gross," I said.

"You can't join our forority," Krista said.

Cara spat at his feet. We ran away. I looked back, just for a second. I could only see his shadow. It was crouched over, like maybe he had fallen. Maybe he was throwing up.

NICOLE TOOK HER SHIRT OFF FIRST

We decided we'd do it at Jason's on Friday, at 6:45. His mom never got home until nine at the earliest, so we figured that was plenty of time. And, I don't know. We thought 6:45 was funny.

Jason had a bunk bed, the bottom full-size, the top a twin where his little brother slept. We were sitting on the bottom bunk, all five of us, close together, drinking beer and waiting for the numbers on the clock to change. We all kept on saying "six forty-five" and then giggling.

Soon it was 6:44, and then there it was: 6:45. We stopped laughing and looked at each other. Nicole at me, and me at Jason and then Vincent, and Chelsea was looking away. Nicole and I were best friends, and Chelsea was our second best. Jason and Vincent were best friends. Vincent and I were neighbors. We'd all known each other since middle school, and me and Vincent since we were kids. We got so still for a moment.

Nicole took her shirt off first, and then we did the same. We took off our pants, and we sat there, the girls in bras and panties, the boys in boxers. It felt awkward and unsexy, so to speed things along I took off my bra, and then the other girls did too. Nicole leaned in to kiss me. Her mouth was cold from the beer. We broke away, and then I was kissing Jason, and Chelsea had her hand on my thigh. We all kissed and touched and moved around, grabbing onto each other's bodies. But the boys wouldn't take off their boxers, and when Jason went to stick his fingers in my underwear I pushed him away. Except then Nicole and Vincent went into the closet, and then we heard noises, and then neither of them was a virgin anymore. After that, they were boyfriend and girlfriend. After that, they were in love.

◆

Vincent and I had hung out after school most days since he'd moved here in the first grade. When we were little we ran around the neighborhood, reenacting scenes from movies, climbing trees, building forts, throwing rocks. Sometimes I even got him to act out the books I read, the Laurie to my Jo, the Pa to my Laura. We got older. Vincent's mom died. His dad no longer cared what we did. In junior high, we started smoking his cigarettes, sneaking a can or two of his beer. Now we were in tenth grade, and all we did was smoke pot and play *Tekken*. I was only ever good at video games when high.

I'd never thought Vincent was cute or anything. He'd only ever been my friend. He was too skinny for me and looked like a rabbit with his lack of a chin. The rabbitness got worse when he smoked—red eyes, a strange twitchy thing with his mouth. But Nicole said it was weird, her best friend and her boyfriend hanging out together all the time. We both tried to point out that we'd done this since we were kids, tell her about the games we'd played, but that just made her more upset. I stopped going over there unless she was there too.

Things were different now. Nicole liked beer and not weed, so we drank instead of smoked and I didn't play video games. We'd listen to music and just sit there, Nicole flipping through magazines, me sometimes reading a book, Vincent playing *Tekken* by himself. It was boring, mostly, but I didn't like being alone. I would go home before it got dark so Nicole and Vincent could do whatever. So they could fuck.

◆

Nicole went to visit her dad in Seattle for all of June and July. She did that every summer. This year she fought her mom, trying to get out of it so she could stay home with Vincent, but her mom told her you can't argue with a custody arrangement.

With Nicole gone, things between Vincent and me went back to the way they were before: smoking weed, playing video games. Except for when she called. When that happened, we'd press pause and I stayed quiet. He sat on the edge of the bed, his back to me, and I walked around the room, running my fingers over his things, looking at his posters, looking at the back of his head, silent as a ghost, barely there. He still had the baseball glove he'd gotten signed by Tony Gwynn in third grade, the medal we'd won in sixth grade for Science Olympiad, an identical one dangling from my bedpost next door. Besides that, everything in his room was different, had been replaced, now the bedroom of a teenager, not a child.

◆

It was almost August. Vincent told me he had something special when I called that day before I came over. When I got there, we smoked a bowl and then he pulled out a fifth of Jack from his closet.

"I stole it for us," he said and smiled.

"You know I can't play *Tekken* drunk," I said.

"But I've been saving it."

"For what?"

"I don't know," he said. "A bon voyage to video games?" He looked disappointed, so I told him we could play until I got too fucked-up. We poured shots.

I beat him three times in a row. Then I lost, and lost again. "I'm too drunk," I said.

Vincent put down his controller. "Let's take another shot." He was drunker than me, and slurring.

I didn't want one but I took it anyway. I clinked my glass against his, spilling a trail of whiskey on his dresser.

"Look at that," he said, and pointed to the clock in the VCR. "It's almost six forty-five."

He was right. It was 6:44.

"Can I have a kiss for old times' sake?"

"Fuck you," I said. I didn't mean it.

"Come on, just a little one?" He was tilting toward me, the drunk look coating his eyes, but underneath there was something more vulnerable, like he was afraid what would happen if I said no. I pecked him on the mouth. It meant nothing.

Except it didn't feel like nothing.

My heart was beating fast and we pulled away and looked at each other. Then we were kissing again, but this time with tongue, and the next thing I knew we were on the floor.

◆

We swore to each other we wouldn't tell Nicole. It would devastate her, we agreed, but I think she might have known something was going on anyway. I would go to his house and she would be there and it would be normal, except things could shift so quickly. His knee might be out as I was walking by and I'd graze it with my wrist, just for a second, the kind of thing we'd never given any thought before. But now we pulled apart so quick you'd think we'd snapped in half. Or Nicole would leave the room, to pee, to get some water, and we'd sit in a heavy silence that hurt.

◆

I was sitting in my room, a few days before Christmas, listening to music and reading. My phone rang. I picked it up.

"Bitch," she said. There was a click, and then dial tone.

◆

Christmas break ended and I didn't know where to sit at lunch, because Chelsea wouldn't talk to me either. I'd see the four of them across the quad—Chelsea and Jason were dating now—and you'd never have known there was a person missing. I could have started hanging out with other people, I guess—it wasn't like I had no friends, but it seemed too difficult, too tiresome, so most days I went to the edge of campus and ate my sandwich in the bushes with a book between my knees. The weekends were long and lonely.

◆

I was doing homework when someone knocked on my bedroom door. Instead of being Mom or Dad, in walked Chelsea and Nicole. I froze at first, but I figured they couldn't do much with my parents just down the hallway.

"Hi," I said, and the word hung there.

Chelsea shut the door. Nicole was standing so close to me. I could smell her perfume—Thierry Mugler Angel, same as before. It made me miss her. I'd really missed her. I hadn't been in the same room as her for almost three months.

"Are you sorry?" she said.

"Of course I'm sorry," I said. "I was sorry the second it happened. It was so stupid and I don't understand why—"

"Good," she said, cutting me off. "I'm not mad anymore, I decided. Let's go drive around and get high. Chelsea has her dad's van."

My mom was in the kitchen, cleaning up from dinner. "I'm going out with Nicole and Chelsea for a little bit," I told her on our way out.

"Have fun!" she said. Normally my mom would want to know when I'd be back, but you could tell she was just thrilled to see me with my old friends. She never said anything, but I knew she'd wondered where they'd disappeared to.

Nicole gave me shotgun, and she got in the back seat. Chelsea drove to the end of the cul-de-sac and pulled over. "We'll just smoke right here," she said. We both climbed in the back with Nicole. It was one of those VW vans with the seats facing each other like in a living room.

"Do you have any weed?" Chelsea said.

"No." I didn't know I was supposed to bring any.

"It's okay," Nicole said. "We have some."

"Cool," I said.

We sat there. No one got out weed or a pipe. "Are you ready?" Nicole said finally. She was smiling, but she looked pissed.

She punched me before I could answer. At first I didn't

know what had happened. My head whacked the side of the van. Things went black, and then very bright, and then the world stilled for a second. My eyes were watering and my nose dripped blood. Nicole was laughing at me. My head began to throb.

I could hear the door slide open. "Get the fuck out," Nicole said, and I did, stumbling, catching my foot on a seat belt, one hand over my nose.

"Whore," she said, and spat at me. She missed, and it landed at my feet. The sun was almost down, and some of the blood from my nose dripped through my fingers, and I watched it fall, landing so it mixed with her spit.

THE OTHER TIME A GROWN MAN THREATENED MY LIFE

There was this weird hippie guy who hung around the Palms. He owned a van and a llama and not much else. We called him Van Man. I didn't know the name of the llama. The two of them slept in the van every night at the far end of the parking lot, Van Man in the driver's seat, llama in the back. He'd cut out panels in the van so the llama could stick its head out. It didn't seem like a very comfortable living arrangement, but what did I know?

One day I was working the cash register at the bookstore when Van Man came into the store with the llama. He walked right over to the magazines, the lead for the llama wrapped loosely around his fingers like he was holding a balloon. It was dead silent for a second, a thick communal shock, everyone staring at the man and his llama. The moment passed, and everyone began talking over one another at once. A fucking llama. In a fucking bookstore.

I really liked my manager, this nice guy with a trendy beard who'd gotten me into Bret Easton Ellis, but when he told Van Man to get out of the bookstore, he seemed like nothing more than a spineless little bitch. "Come on," my manager said. "Let's be cool. Take the llama out of the store."

"There's not a sign," Van Man said. And it was true. There wasn't. There was a sign that said NO DOGS but it mentioned nothing about cats or rabbits or llamas. But there wasn't a sign about how you weren't allowed to bomb the store or light the books on fire or jerk off in the erotica section (which had happened before) either.

My manager left to call security. Everyone was just standing around, staring, as Van Man paged through the new issue of *Maxim*. A few minutes later, the security guard showed up. He was a pathetic man, pink and doughy. My friends and I all worked in the shopping center—the bagel store, the Meineke, the sandwich shop—and when we got off work, we met up at the tables in front of the movie theater to talk and smoke, waste time until there was something better to do, somebody's parents out of town, a bonfire at the beach. We knew all the security guards. We called this one Tweety because of his car, a yellow RAV4 with a Tweety Bird sticker on the window and a Tweety Bird tire cover and a personalized TWTYBRD license plate. It was impossible to take him seriously ever—not when he yelled at us for drinking or smoking or making too much noise. The worst he could do was order us off the property. When that happened, we walked across the drop-off area to do the same things we did at the tables but in front of the stop sign instead.

"You gotta go," he told Van Man.

"Whatever, man," Van Man said, like some stoned guy in some stoner movie. "I'm just reading a magazeeeeeeeen."

"You gotta get the llama out of here," Tweety told him, and pulled on his arm, the one that wasn't holding the llama lead.

That pissed Van Man off. He started flailing his arms, which yanked on the llama lead, which made the llama let out a long weird snort like a horse. But finally he relented, petted the llama on the nose to settle it down, allowed himself to be escorted out of the store. They were at the door when Tweety told him, "And don't you come back," trying too hard to play a role.

Van Man laughed, like he had the exact same thought as me. "Hope this makes you feel real big, mister badgey-badgey five-dollars-an-hour man," he said. "Mister badgey five-dollar fake pig."

I couldn't help it. I started laughing. I tried to stop, ring up the customer, a middle-aged woman buying a Dean Koontz novel. She seemed shook-up, clutching the shitty book. I couldn't. "Sorry," I told her, beeping the book under the scanner. I was still laughing when I gave her the change.

When I got off work, I went right up to the circle, sat down in one of the metal chairs, told the guys who were sitting there all about it. Mister badgey-badgey five-dollars-an-hour man. And from then on, that's what we said to Tweety whenever he told us to be quiet or settle down or put away that beer.

♦

The security guards all came and went, working at the Palms for a couple months or a year before disappearing, nearly indistinguishable from one another. Useless doughy guys with buzz cuts, weak rejects from the actual police, who rode around the shopping center in a golf cart because they were too fat and lazy to walk. Tweety had only stood out because of his car.

But one day, there was a new security guard at the Palms, different than all the rest. He was giant, nearly seven feet tall, and gorgeous in a scary way, cheekbones and angles, a shaved head that was almost sculptural. The first time I saw him I felt scared in a way I couldn't explain. I'd just gotten off work when he walked around the corner. The security guards had these sticklike things they held up to various receivers around the shopping center until they beeped, I guess to ensure they were doing their rounds. He came around the corner, big and muscular and scowling, beeping his wand. His hair was so short you could see the perfect shape of his skull.

Later that day, Colin, who was always around, Chandra, my best friend, and I were smoking a joint in the corridor behind the movie theater when we heard someone yelling. I stood up, looking over the low stucco wall we were crouching behind. I saw Van Man getting yelled at by the new security guard. "You get the fuck off this property," the security guard was saying. Van Man was standing outside his van, next to the llama's head peeking out. I waited for him to say something but he didn't. Instead, Van Man walked around the van, opened the door, got in the driver's seat. I heard the van turn on, *put-put-put*. I watched him drive out of the parking lot, around the hill, until he drove out of sight. The new security guard continued his rounds, walking. I never once saw him in the golf cart.

♦

The new security guard ignored us for a long time, didn't say a word as we sat at the circle and smoked. One day, though, it was the release of the latest installment of a movie franchise, and the space in front of the theater, our space, was packed. Someone had a big bottle of store-brand vodka, and we were passing it around, pouring it into soda cups. We were about to head out to one of the dirt lots that had appeared by the side of the new freeway, waiting to be turned into another subdivision, one of our go-tos when there was nowhere else to party.

We didn't notice him at first. One minute nobody was there, and the next minute there he was, standing behind Colin, confusing because of his size. Colin was holding the bottle, pouring it into his can of Pepsi. The new security guard put his hands on Colin's chair, one on each side of his neck. Colin was an asshole, didn't care about respecting anybody, but he froze. The security guard's eyes were blue and sharp like crystals. His face was completely expressionless. I couldn't tell if he actually cared or if he was just doing his job. "Put the bottle away," he said, quiet and calm, but there was something buried underneath his words that chilled me.

I wondered what Colin would do. Normally he'd make fun of the security guard, give him shit. But he just put the cap on the bottle, handed it to somebody, who put it in their backpack.

The security guard took his hands off the chair. As he walked away, I noticed something peeking up over his blue uniform collar. Fine black lines, uneven in color. I didn't know a whole lot but it looked like a prison tattoo, the tip of an Iron Cross.

♦

I was sitting at the chairs, waiting for Chandra to arrive. There was an old paper sitting on one of the far tables and I didn't have anything better to do, so I walked over and picked it up, paged through it. A headline caught my eye, buried toward the back of the paper.

OCEAN BEACH VICTIM WAS COLORFUL
LOCAL KNOWN AS THE "LLAMA MAN"

The article was about Van Man. The Llama Man was Van Man. He was dead, had been found drowned twenty miles south in OB, weights on his ankles and rocks in his pockets. A suicide note had been left in the sand. He was bipolar, the article said. He'd given away the llama a few days earlier to a guy in the neighboring county with a farm. This was a week ago, shortly after the new security guard told Van Man to leave. I didn't think he'd been murdered or anything as conspiratorial as that, but I still felt as though the security guard had something to do with it, had been one of the final straws that damned Van Man to his death.

◆

A couple weeks later, it was a Friday but there wasn't anything to do. It was the weekend after Thanksgiving, and a lot of people were busy or out of town so there was a smaller group than usual, maybe fifteen of us, trying to figure out where we could go. Finally we decided on the beach. There were few enough of us that the cops probably wouldn't come. None of us were old enough to buy alcohol except for Colin. We pooled together money, and there was only enough for a case of beer and a pint of cheap vodka but that was fine. We handed the money to Colin. "I lost my ID," he said.

"What?" I said.

"Yeah, I lost it."

"Shit."

"Don't worry about it," he said. Then he disappeared with the money. Maybe he was going to steal it. Maybe he knew someone working at the gas station. But he came back empty-handed.

"What the fuck?"

"Be patient," Colin said. He had a little smile on his

face, the way he did when he'd come up with a good scam. When nobody was looking a few minutes later, he waved at me to follow him. We walked behind the theater to his car, a beat-up maroon IROC-Z with broken windows that wouldn't roll down. It reeked in that car, from Colin always hotboxing it with cigarettes due to the broken windows. We got in the car and drove around the corner to the alley. I was just about to ask Colin what we were doing when the new security guard walked up. He was carrying a case of Miller Lite and a paper bag. He handed it to Colin, who got out of the car to put it in the trunk. I watched them bump fists in the rearview. "Thanks, Derrick," Colin said, the first time I heard his name. The security guard, Derrick, said nothing to me, simply looked back at me with a face full of hatred, like he knew I possessed some despicable secret.

◆

This happened a few more times—Derrick buying us beer—until eventually he started partying with us. It was another lame night, nowhere to go, so we just went across the street to Beer Woo, this vacant lot that was supposed to turn into another shopping center but was empty for years instead, due to some boring fight with the city council. It was higher than the shopping center and nobody ever seemed to notice us, which felt a little magical, hiding in the camouflage of plain sight. Derrick had two cases of beer, Miller Lite again, and also a bottle of Jameson. We walked across the street and he didn't say anything, and I was starting to think he was just straight-up mean. But when we got to Beer Woo, he asked me for a cigarette and I gave him one and then he handed me the bottle of Jameson. I opened it, but I didn't have anything to drink out of, and I was afraid he'd yell at me if I put my mouth on the bottle. He seemed to notice, some animallike intuition. "Go on," he said. "Take a sip."

I took a pull from the bottle. It burned. I handed it back to him, and he took a sip too, his mouth touching the same part of the bottle as mine. I knew there was logically no meaning in that but I still felt violated, knowing a part of myself was now a part of him too, a weird thrill.

He asked me for a light so I pulled out my lighter. He tried to do the thing that creepy guys always do, making you light their cigarette, or the reverse, so there was no choice but to be close to their body. I pretended not to notice, placed the lighter in his hand. "You can keep it," I said, even though it was the only one I had. I walked away, pretended to just notice Chandra, hugged her like I hadn't last seen her a few minutes ago.

"What are you doing?" she said.

"He creeps me out," I said.

"Who? Derrick?"

"Shhh," I said. "I don't want him to hear."

Chandra looked at me, confused. She seemed to think Derrick was fine, no different than the rest of us.

◆

Derrick came out with us a lot after that. I learned that he lived in El Cajon, thirty minutes away and one of the shittiest places to live in San Diego County. In San Diego, everyone said that anywhere that wasn't the coast was filled with white supremacists—El Cajon, Santee/Klan-tee, Spring Valley, Lakeside. Racists. El Cajon was the shittiest of them all. At least Santee looked like a generic Southern California suburb, with tree-lined streets and the big Costco. El Cajon, on the other hand, was hot, poor, and ugly.

It didn't matter, though, because Derrick was an actual racist. A skinhead. He listened to horrible music, racist punk and racist death metal. The lines I'd seen on his neck were indeed a prison tattoo, or at least that's what he said, eighteen months in San Quentin. Of course it was San Quentin. There was another tattoo on his chest, which I saw when he took off his uniform, two lightning bolts like a regular fucking Nazi.

I didn't know if I believed him. He never gave details about what his crimes entailed, wouldn't tell us why he was sent to prison. But mostly I didn't believe him because I couldn't imagine a security guard firm in Santa Bonita hiring a felon.

Nobody seemed to care except me, including Chandra, who was half Mexican. Derrick didn't seem to notice her eyes or her skin or her last name, Martinez. Chandra didn't seem to notice either, the bad music or the bad tattoos. The two of them even made out one time. When we talked about it later, she didn't even care. "What?" she said. "He's hot."

"He's a fucking skinhead," I said, but for some unfathomable reason, Chandra didn't believe me, as though the tattoos and music and shaved head were random aberrations.

We were running this scam at Home Depot. One of us would go in, buy a spindle of wire that cost twenty bucks. The scam was that we'd steal one of the barcodes from the fiber optics cables that looked the same but cost five times as much. We'd peel off the original barcode, replace it with the stolen one. Then we'd drive to another Home Depot, return it, and pocket the difference. Home Depot gave you cash on returns, didn't even want to see an ID. With the money, we bought beer and a room at the Motel 6 off the freeway. Eventually we got greedy, started to return two spindles instead of one, buy cocaine and kegs instead of just beer. The parties at the Motel 6 got so wild that we had to get a new person to rent the room each time because we left them so trashed.

It was late, maybe 4:00 a.m. We'd been doing lines of coke all night at the Motel 6. It brought that weird thing in the air, tense and thick. We ran out of drugs and Derrick didn't know we were low and he got mad. All of a sudden he was yelling, indecipherable. His eyes were bloodshot and red. I guess a lot of the coke money had been his and he was mad it was gone.

"Dude," Colin said. "You got to quiet down."

Usually Colin was the one Derrick liked best, but that just pissed him off. I watched him get up, walk over to the shitty desk, and pick up an empty beer bottle. He stood there for a moment, frozen, before breaking the bottle on the edge of the desk. "You stole it," he said, walking over to me, the broken bottle over his head.

I sat up from the bed. I had no idea why he was blaming me. I didn't feel scared, for some reason. He looked so stupid, a big dumb boy, with big-dumb-boy tattoos. The look in his eyes was dull and blank and I was tiny and didn't know how to fight, but still I felt like I could take him, somehow. I wanted to laugh at him, to tell him he was a stupid boy, but that didn't exactly seem like the best move. So I just sat there, staring at him, his stupid cold blue eyes, and it felt like everything was both pulsing and frozen.

"Dude," Colin said. "Everything is chill."

Derrick turned to him, as though he had forgotten what he was doing. He dropped the broken bottle on the floor. I thought for a second that he'd calmed down. He walked over to the TV. He picked it up. He tried throwing it but it was still plugged into the wall. It yanked out when he threw it, but instead of launching in the air, it tumbled right down onto his feet. The TV broke with a pop. He screamed, high-pitched, like a little girl.

None of us knew what to do. When it came down to it, we were just nice suburban teens. We didn't break TVs. Something seemed to shake loose from Derrick in that moment, all of us standing there, silent and horrified. He started laughing. "Shit," he said. "I went a little crazy."

Chandra and I left the hotel room after that. I wasn't sober enough to drive but I had to get out of there. We took the coast home, thinking I'd be less likely to get pulled over that way.

We were up on the hill, right before the stoplight closest to my neighborhood, when I saw something in the middle of the road. I noticed it just in time. It was a boulder, a big chunk of sandstone from the cliffs above. We got out of the car. The night was dead silent and there was a bit of fog rolling in from the coast, everything washed out in the yellow of the streetlight.

Chandra and I were able to move it, just barely, out into the other lane. The sandstone got all over my hands, stained my jeans.

◆

After the TV incident, we tried to stay away from Derrick, no longer invited him out, but sometimes he went up to the circle when he got off work anyway, came out with us uninvited. I did my best to ignore him, stay out of his way. I think he noticed. He was always staring at me, like everything was all my fault.

◆

It was morning, way too bright, but I was sitting at the Palms anyway. It had been a long night and I was still too jacked up to go home. My mom was always threatening to drug test me, and if I failed the drug test, she'd kick me out, so I was staying away from home more and more. After checkout time at Motel 6, I had Colin drop me off here, until I could sober up and walk home.

I'd been sitting there for a few minutes, elbows on my lap, head hanging down, trying to get my bearings though it was hard in the hot sun, when I heard someone yelling. It sounded like a mess of nonsense except for two distinct words: *fucking bitch.*

I looked up, feeling dazed. The light was splotchy. I saw Derrick, maybe fifty feet away, walking toward me. He had a cup from Subway in his hand, was dressed in jeans, his security guard shirt on but unbuttoned. He started screaming at me. I had no idea why. I'd done nothing to him. He was calling me a bitch and a cunt, a stupid bitch, a dumb fucking cunt. He stayed across the pavilion though, away from me, which was confusing, like he was afraid of me. I didn't say anything to him because it seemed so insane. I was just sitting there, hungover and tired.

Me not saying anything seemed to piss him off more. He started saying he was going to kill me. "I'll murder you, bitch. I'll bury your body in a shallow grave. You'll rot, bitch." He threw the soda cup at me but missed. I watched the ice splatter on the cement.

I didn't know what to do. It all seemed so wildly illogical. I couldn't help but imagine my decaying body, bugs eating my eyeballs.

I grabbed my purse without looking at him. I walked

down to the bookstore, went into the break room, used the phone. I asked my mom to pick me up, waiting for her in the safety of the bookstore, looking out the window the whole time, just in case. When I got in the car, she said nothing about the way I smelled or the way I was acting.

We never saw Derrick again. All I know is he got fired. I don't know why. I didn't tell on him. That wasn't how my friends treated it, though. They acted like I did it, like I'd conquered him, like I'd done something, anything, like I'd won.

AUTOMOTIVE SAFETY

I kept on almost getting in trouble. The first time, I stopped at the 7-Eleven near my house after work. I bought a pack of cigarettes and a candy bar. I got back in my car, stopped at the red light. Something felt wrong. I'd sat at that light a hundred times before: stucco buildings, palm trees, Mexican restaurant, sidewalk. That night, everything looked off, like somebody had placed the buildings crooked. I looked at the road, the painted lines. I was inside them. I was just tired, I decided, near delirious. I waited for the light to turn green. It looked so far away.

Red lights flashing behind my car. The cops. I thought for sure they weren't after me because I'd done nothing wrong. My headlights were on and my tags were up to date and I wasn't speeding. But the cop kept following me, so I finally pulled over, the road near the beachside campground. There were no streetlights and that stretch of road was so dark. There was an empty beer bottle in my cup holder from yesterday and I did my best to hide it covertly under my seat. I got the bottle out of view just as soon as the cop knocked on my window.

He shined his flashlight right in my face and I blinked. I handed over my license and registration.

"Do you know why I pulled you over?" he asked, looking at my license. He was fat and hairless.

"No," I said. I felt a little indignant. I'd done nothing wrong.

"You were driving on the wrong side of the road."

"What," I said. That was why the light had looked so far away. I was a fucking moron.

"I'm so sorry, officer," I said. "I'm so sorry, I didn't realize, I've been working doubles at work and I'm just really brain-dead and tired." This was all true.

The cop stared at my face. I was pretty sure I looked appropriately sober and tired, dressed in a black button-down, an innocent restaurant employee, but then he told me to get out of the car. *Fuck*, I thought. I'd had a glass of wine before I left work, dumped in a coffee mug, and I was taking a lot of pills around then but I hadn't had any that day. I was pretty sure I'd be fine but I wasn't positive.

I still had my apron in my lap and I forgot. It fell on the ground when I stood up and all my pens spilled out, my corkscrew. "Fuck," I said.

"You can pick those up when we're done here," the cop said. He made me walk in a straight line and was about to have me do something else, I hoped it wasn't the backward alphabet because I couldn't do that. But then his radio crackled, somebody saying a series of numbers.

"You can go," he told me. No ticket, no warning.

"Okay," I said. I walked back to my car. I picked up my pens. He drove away. I didn't get in trouble.

◆

The next day, I opened the restaurant up with Ally. I hated Ally. She was a real bitch to everyone who was, in her mind, beneath her: the kitchen staff, the kitchen manager, the bussers, the hostesses, and me, the cashier. But to the other servers, and the front-house managers, she smiled and laughed and cracked jokes. None of those people noticed the discrepancy, but the rest of us did. The kitchen staff had their own nickname for her, Perra Grande. Big Bitch. Because Ally was big, like six feet tall, and a bitch.

I went to the kitchen with a plastic bin to stock the cooler. That was one of my jobs, besides getting the servers change from the till and doing to-go orders. I was also the bartender. All we served was beer and wine, so that meant I opened and poured bottles. The restaurant was a chain and had strict rules about pouring wine. I had to fill each glass to an imaginary line, the least you could possibly pour and still call it a full glass. I had to keep track of everything, and if I didn't get five and a half glasses out of every bottle, I'd get in trouble. But this meant there was 0.16 of a glass unaccounted for in each bottle. That 0.16 is what I drank after work, mixing white and red, whatever was left, it didn't matter, it was basically rosé, I figured.

I filled the bin with the wine bottles and the beer bottles

and the beer glasses. It was heavy and Lolo offered to carry it. Lolo was smaller than me but strong. He was my favorite of all the kitchen staff. He taught me the best insults: *chupa mi pinche verga, me cago en tu madre, no mames güey.* When the restaurant closed, I sometimes gave him a cup of stolen wine.

Lolo put the bin on the counter. He looked out at the restaurant and Ally was sitting there, folding napkins. He clicked his tongue. I gave him a look. We laughed. Ally didn't acknowledge us.

The to-go orders were hell that day. I had a giant corporate order: eighteen pizzas, twelve salads, four appetizers. The restaurant was one of those fancy pizza places, with a wood-fired oven, where a tiny pizza cost fifteen dollars. We were right near a bunch of office parks and got orders like this all the time. I had to label everything with my Sharpie. I had to make sure the dressing lids were on tight, count out the bread, count out the tiny tubs of butter. This order wanted me to label everything with a name, which was ridiculous. But corporate orders always tipped the best, so I did everything they asked.

And in the meantime I had the regular to-go orders and getting the servers their drinks. It was a lot at once, but I was good at it. I enjoyed the chaos, the need to make each movement count. And I loved being the cashier. I made less in tips but it didn't matter because I didn't have to deal with customers. I took their credit cards, I told them thank you, and that's about it. I didn't even know who ate the food I put in the bags, if the pizza and salad and pasta was for a family of four or a single person binge-eating in a dark bedroom.

All the servers knew to stay off my computer during the lunch rush. All the servers knew the slightest interruption would throw me off. I was almost done with the big order and then another came in and I went to enter it, but Ally was on my fucking computer, typing in substitutions.

"Can you get off my computer?" I said.

"One sec," she said. She deleted something, started over.

"I really need that," I said.

"I'm almost done," she said. She didn't look at me.

The corporate-order person showed up then, a young guy in a polo shirt. He was a few minutes early and the one thing I hadn't done yet was count out the forks.

"Your order's almost ready," I told him and smiled. My work voice was something you might use with a kindergartner, high-pitched and slow, and my smile was big and effective. The only thing I couldn't change was the look in my eyes. I was pretty sure my work smile looked psychotic, but none of the customers seemed to notice.

"There are forty of us," the young guy said in an irritated voice.

"Yes, thank you," I said. As if I didn't fucking know, buddy, by the forty names I had to write on everything, including the ones where two people were sharing.

I went to print their order but Ally was still using my computer. It was like she was taking as long as she could on purpose. She was ruining my tip, I could feel it. Tips on to-go orders had nothing to do with logic, if I was good at my job. They were based on something like energy, and with Ally on that computer, I could feel the energy getting thrown off. She finally finished typing and I rang up the order, a platinum Amex. In the tip line, he wrote *0*, which always felt like a big "Fuck you, I didn't forget to tip, I'm purposely giving you nothing." And then the next person came in, and I hadn't even rung in their salad because of fucking Ally.

Lolo was working the salad station and had seen what happened. He gave me a look that said *I got you* and made that salad fast. But the person still had to wait. They didn't tip me either.

When the customer was gone, I walked over to the salad station and said, "Perra Grande puede chupar mí culo."

Lolo said, "No, Perra Grande puede chupar *mí* culo," and then we laughed.

The to-go orders slowed down so I started running food for the servers. I was gone for a couple minutes and when I came back, Ally was pouring a glass of chardonnay. The servers weren't supposed to do that. The glass she was pouring was way over the line. I didn't say anything. I wanted to rat her out to the manager, but I wouldn't do that either. When she walked past me on her way out of my little corner, I mumbled at her, "Dumb bitch."

"What did you say?" Ally said.

"Huh?" I said.

"What did you say to me?" Ally said.

I told her she must be hearing things and then I rang up another order.

I made almost nothing in tips that day. And then I went to my car. Someone had been breaking into employees' cars. All of us—the Starbucks employees, the bookstore, the other restaurants—had to park in the bottom level of the garage. It was mostly stereos, sometimes packs of cigarettes, tip money, a GPS. It was really rude—the wealthy customers' BMWs and Mercedes, parked in the upper levels, were left alone. But our Civics and Tercels and old Volvos all got broken into. Every day, I took the faceplate off my stereo and put it in my purse. But that day I'd forgotten. That day, my stereo was gone, just an empty square in my dashboard. One more fuck-you from the day. Thanks a lot.

◆

I was closing the restaurant, another double shift. I'd done three back-to-back again. I felt horrible, a little in my legs but mostly in my mood, like my ability to feign niceness had been exhausted. I couldn't smile at any more strangers. It was impossible.

I usually didn't take pills until I got home, but I couldn't bring myself to count the till and do the cleanup with just a little wine. When nobody was looking, I pulled out my silver pill case and swallowed one Oxy and one Klonopin.

I started feeling sleepy on the way home. I didn't feel high yet, I was pretty sure—just all the back-to-back doubles, just tired. I felt my eyes beginning to droop. I hadn't gotten a new stereo yet so I had no music to blast me awake. I rolled down the window, let the smoggy night air hit me in the face. The air was warm. It didn't help much.

I was about a block away from my house when I felt something violent. I'd fallen asleep. My car had run something over. I had felt the bang and the bump and it'd woken me up.

My car was on the curb. There was something lumpy under it but the street was dark and I couldn't quite see what it was. I imagined a child, a person, dying.

I was about to just pull my car off the curb and drive the rest of the way home, do a hit-and-run, but I couldn't do it. I opened my door and got out of the car.

My bumper was a little dented but that was it. The thing I'd run over was some mailboxes. Their thin spikes had gotten demolished by my car.

I didn't know what I was supposed to do. It was eleven at night, too late to go knocking on doors. I didn't want to call the police, obviously. I felt like I needed to clean up the mess and maybe take the broken stakes and the dented mailboxes and throw them in a dumpster somewhere, but I knew things with mail could be federal crimes and I didn't want to commit a federal crime. I just backed up my car, drove away. I figured the next morning before work, I'd go to the mailboxes and look at the addresses and apologize to the owners, offer to buy them new mailboxes or something. At least it wasn't a dead kid.

But the next morning, the mailboxes were gone. It had happened in front of an apartment complex with all the doors turned in on one another, impossible to tell which apartment each of the mailboxes might have belonged to without going to each one, which seemed insane. I just went to work.

I got there really early. None of the servers were there yet, just the kitchen staff. I went to fill up the cooler with the glasses and bottles. Lolo wasn't there to help me. I realized I hadn't seen him in a while.

I went into the big fridge with all the bins of lettuce and meat and the giant jars of ranch. Tomás, the kitchen manager, was in there, taking inventory with a clipboard.

"Hey," I said. "Where's Lolo?"

Tomás put the clipboard down. "He's gone," he said.

"What?" I said.

"He's back in Mexico," he said.

"Oh my god," I said. "That's so unfair." I don't know what I expected Tomás to say, maybe for him to just shrug or tell me there was some kind of raid. But instead he looked at the open fridge door, like he was making sure nobody could eavesdrop.

"No," Tomás said, lowering his voice. "You know how everybody's car was getting broken into?"

"Yeah," I said, trying to put this information together. Lolo's . . . stereo got stolen? And then he reported it to the cops?

"That was Lolo," he said.

It didn't compute. "What?" I said.

"Lolo," Tomás said. "He's the one who was stealing the stereos."

Lolo, my friend. He'd stolen my fucking stereo.

♦

The lunch rush was crazy, as usual, two corporate orders that day, and I felt like an octopus, something with a freak-ish number of arms in perfect rhythm—the bread, the salad dressing, the bags, the credit card slips, and the servers' beer and wine. I loved it when that happened. I tried to forget about Lolo. When I became a machine, an hour slipped away like nothing. An order of wine came in the machine, and I put a salad in a bag with bread, and then I went to grab the wine from the cooler below me.

Except there was a big rat in the fridge already, Ally's stupid giant head, rifling through the bottles to get her own wine.

I got so mad. She couldn't wait one fucking second. It was instinctual, unthinking. I took the open door and slammed it against her head.

"Ahhhh," Ally yelled. "What the fuck?"

"Oh my god," I said. "I'm so sorry. I didn't see you there." I clapped my hand over my mouth in fake surprise. "I'm so sorry. Here, let me get you that wine."

I poured her the glass. She was rubbing her forehead, where it had hit against the rim of the little fridge. I could see a knot forming already.

"Oh my god," I said again. "Let me get you some ice."

"It's fine," Ally said. I couldn't tell if she knew I'd done it on purpose. She grabbed the wineglass and brought it to her table.

I was paranoid the rest of the day, worried that Ally would tattle on me. Later I saw her talking to my manager and I thought she was ratting me out but nothing happened. I got away with it.

I left work right as the sun was going down. The traffic was always heavy but that day it was worse than usual. I didn't care. I had brought an old boom box in my car, and I had my iPod plugged into it and the music was loud. I sat in my car, not moving, smoking a cigarette, drinking a little cup of wine, and everything was good, like I was just chilling in my bedroom. I finally crawled to the overpass and from there I could see down onto the other freeway.

There was a giant wreck under me. A semi had T-boned an SUV. The SUV was demolished, upside down, a crumpled clump of metal. It looked like it had just happened, no cop cars or ambulances. It looked like someone was surely dead. It was a really bad accident.

I tried to look down, see the dead bodies, but the road cut off my view. Then I saw a lick of flames and the rest of it caught on fire quick. The smoke was black and heavy and it rose up around my car, glorious and chaotic. I knew somebody was dead and I should feel bad but I didn't. I loved the fire and I loved the smoke and I loved the sunset, how everything was vibrating and vivid, the way the disaster below me made my life in that car feel so bright and loud. I heard sirens, I saw flashing lights. A fire truck, three cop cars, two ambulances. No cars were moving. We were all just sitting there, exhausts pumping pointless fumes into the atmosphere, destroying the earth.

People started doing the thing where they get out of their cars, as if that would do something, as if that satisfied anything, as if there was anything more to see. But I realized there was. I got out of my car too. I looked down through the chain-link fence at the accident. I saw some blond hair, some blood, glitters of broken glass. But then the traffic started moving again and I got back in my car. I drove away. I tried to see the accident in my rearview but there was nothing except a few wisps of smoke.

♦

The next day my shift didn't start until four. The restaurant was empty except there were a bunch of servers sitting on the benches, crying.

"What happened?" I asked. Maybe they were crying over Lolo.

But then they told me it was Ally, she was dead, her SUV had gotten T-boned by a semi the day before, on her way home from work. I wanted to laugh but I didn't.

"Oh my god," I said. "That's so sad." I was playacting, the same way I had yesterday when I'd slammed Ally's head in the cooler door. I used the same tone of voice. I said the same words. "Oh my god," I said again. "I'm so sorry." I clapped my hand over my mouth.

I didn't know what I was supposed to do after that. I stood there for a second, putting a sad look on my face. Then I left, to stock the cooler like usual. It seemed way sadder that there was no Lolo to help me, that he had stolen my stereo.

I found out exactly what happened throughout the shift, in between the dinner to-gos and everybody lying about what a good person she was. She wasn't wearing her seat belt. She was always so generous. She'd died before the fire started, her head smacking against steel when the SUV rolled over. She was such a sweetheart. She was on her way to pick up her little brother from day care. The semi driver was drunk. Such a good person. So nice.

I wanted Lolo there, so we could tell the truth. But there was no Lolo. When nobody was looking, I smiled. Big Bitch was dead.

STATE OF EMERGENCY

Adam and I were on the roof. We'd broken up six weeks ago, but most of that time he spent on tour. He hadn't found a new apartment. The band had come back early—the storm. That's why he was there. And also we were doing that thing you aren't supposed to do. Prolonging the breakup.

There was a bunch of shit on the roof. A deflated soccer ball, a trash can, a plastic horse that looked like it came from a carousel, two traffic cones, a busted boom box, and three filthy patio chairs. None of it belonged to us, but none of it belonged to anybody. We'd knocked on the doors of the other apartments, just to check. It didn't take long. There were only three, total, all of us living there somewhat illegally, in an old factory on an industrial street, a weird area that was adjacent to, but not technically in any of, the three trendiest neighborhoods in Brooklyn.

I looked down over the roof, mechanically forced myself to not imagine jumping off. The dumpster was directly below me. I picked up a traffic cone, threw it over. It made a satisfying *thwack* as it hit the garbage. When I worked at the wine store, back in California, it was my job to throw out empty bottles from the tastings. I always threw them in one by one, hard, the bottles bursting off the metal sides of the dumpster, the anger I held in my chest subsiding with each pop of broken glass.

Now I'd been sober for two years. The anger had shifted, still present but lower grade, more persistent. It had gotten worse with the breakup, this swift kick to my life. I threw the other cone over. I threw the boom box, as hard as I could onto the concrete. It shattered. Adam and I looked at each other, laughing. He threw over a plastic chair, too light to stay on course, and it bounced next to the boom box before splintering a leg. It felt like a naughty game, one we'd cloaked in practicality.

Adam carried the plastic horse down the stairs. It was dirty and disgusting but he wanted to keep it. He put the horse in the band's van, parked at the curb. We picked up the broken chair off the street, the largest shards of the boom box, put them in the dumpster, slammed the lid shut. There was no latch and it seemed like it'd blow open but it was better than the roof, at least reducing the element of gravity.

We went back into the apartment, formerly "ours," now just mine and Anna's. Adam had given me his portion of rent while he was gone. All his clothes and records and the guitar and spare drums were exactly where they had been, like nothing had changed. Even our interactions while he'd been gone held the same routine—texting all day until he went dead silent in the evenings when he got to the show. Or at least that's what he said.

I was worried about making rent, the one true problem I

had with the breakup. But I was good at picking up odd jobs. One time, I got five hundred dollars to pack the belongings of two supposed artists living in a loft near the water. Their apartment was too nice for people whose incomes came solely from art. I considered stealing something from them, a belt buckle, a framed dead butterfly. They'd left me alone for hours, touching all of their things. But in recovery I'd lost the ability to lie or steal, the exact opposite of who I'd been when I did drugs. This newfound pathological honesty had been a big part of our breakup. I told Adam about the time I made out with a classmate, what I really thought of his natural deodorant and the bass player in his band, the intricacies of the petty rage I felt when he failed to keep up with his share of the dishes. And now, none of this mattered. Our issues had become weightless, free to flap around, insignificant.

Anna and I had lined up candles, batteries, and a flashlight on the table. We'd filled the Brita pitcher and bathtub. We'd charged our laptops and phones. Anna was from Texas, the panhandle, and I was from Southern California. We knew nothing about this type of storm, relying on a checklist from the CDC. Adam had gotten back an hour ago. He grew up on the North Carolina coast, remembered the roof.

"We should tape up the window," he said, rifling through the drawers until he found a roll of duct tape.

"The website," Anna said. "It said not to do that."

"We always did it growing up," Adam said. "The glass doesn't get all over the place if it breaks."

The website had stated this was a misconception. The glass didn't care if there was tape or not. What did help was putting up shutters or plywood, but, of course, we didn't have those.

I looked at Anna, trying to gauge if she was annoyed at Adam for being there, for his bad advice. But Anna liked Adam. We taped the window. Adam was always wrong, but what did it matter now? There was only one, taking up the whole wall in the living room.

There was nothing else to do. Adam turned on a movie and we sat on the couch. I opened my laptop, refreshed the weather website, watched the blob that was the storm creep closer. I had a story open, one I was trying to finish. I hadn't gotten very far. During our last fight, the one that led to our breakup, he'd told me he wanted someone who was as successful at their art as he was at his. In my head, I'd laughed, filed the line away for later. A person as successful at their art as he was at his. At the time, though, I'd said nothing, because I couldn't come up with a legitimate argument against him. His band had three albums, was always touring. I'd had exactly two stories published in obscure literary magazines. Still, the thought of it bubbled into a flashing image, me stabbing him, blood, it was so stupid that he was sitting next to me on the couch. Adam got up to make a pot of tea, asked if we wanted some. I didn't drink tea. I never had.

There was a loud knock on the door, *bang-bang-bang.* We all jumped. I tried to remember if I'd done anything illegal, and I hadn't but I still felt a twinge of panic. Anna opened the door. It was two firemen, in fireman suits, not cops. They told us they had to get onto our roof, the small awning accessible only through our living room.

We let them in. One opened our window without asking. He climbed onto the awning in front of the window, just big enough for one person. He was doing something to the cables, pulling out zip ties. The other guy stayed in the living room, taking in the taped X. I looked at him more closely. He was really cute. Adam was just standing there, staring at the ground, a sensitive artist with long lashes and pretty lips, sipping his herbal tea. The fireman was cut and hunky, a tanned beefcake, like he might not actually be a fireman but a stripper.

"Do you want some water or something?" I asked the fireman. I knew he didn't want tea. It felt weird to have a stranger standing there idly in my living room, even, and maybe especially, if he was hot.

"Nah," he said. "I'm fine." He had a thick accent, Staten Island or New Jersey, I didn't know the difference. It made him even hotter. A strapping blue-collar babe. Adam, on the other hand, had sanitized his North Carolina accent while he was still in college, exchanged it for the same bland English people spoke where I was from in California.

"How have you guys been doing?" Anna asked. I looked up. I could tell she thought he was hot too. "Have you been busy?" My mind unspooled a scene from a porn, Adam gone, a couple firemen and two ordinary-looking girls.

"Oh yeah, real busy, we're just—" He was interrupted by the other fireman coming back inside.

"Everything's good, girls," he said, as though he hadn't noticed Adam. This fireman was hot too, broad shoulders and velvety brown eyes. I kept expecting one of them to take off their clothes. I wanted to talk to them, ask them questions, unbutton a collar, unbuckle a belt, but they left before we could say or do anything else.

There was a feeling in the room after they left, the electricity of strapping young men. I looked at Adam and could see he was pretending not to notice the presence of unfamiliar testosterone. There were a couple new zip ties on the roof cables, but everything else looked the same.

The wind picked up, sky darkening from the setting sun and heavy clouds. Anna was asking Adam about the tour. I wished she wouldn't. I was the one who said we should break up, but he had agreed a little too quickly. I knew who he was. He claimed he was a feminist, sex positive. I knew the breakup would allow him to fuck whoever he wanted on tour without even feeling guilty. I didn't care what he had done on tour, not really, but I didn't want to imagine it either. The wind whooshed outside, and I felt like I was in a children's book, like I was being haunted by a ghost. The windows shook. Everything in the room felt too still, Adam's annoying voice. I felt a sudden desperate urge to see the storm. I stood up, grabbed my keys and phone. "Where are you going?" Adam said.

"Outside," I told him. I didn't offer an explanation because

I didn't have one. I just wanted the storm to be something more than a blob on a screen. He followed me down the stairs but when I looked back, he was gone. I went out to the stoop. The door slammed behind me. It was windy, windy, windy, enough that it felt dangerous, a sting on my cheeks. I walked into the street and my shirt billowed in front of me like a sail. I watched the trash and dead leaves lifting in the air, a stray wig, somebody's Halloween costume, a rising nest of bright tangles. The wind was noisy yet it felt calm, no sirens, no honking horns, no passing cars from the BQE, just my own breath in sync with the wind. I felt alone, alone in seeing this laser focus, everything yellowed in the streetlight, and it felt like my life before Adam, when I still did drugs, the way that sometimes everything zoomed into something a little bit sharper than reality. I walked down the block, watched the power lines sway. In my mind I saw one of them snapping, swinging to me, the jolt of electrocution. But nothing happened. I went back inside.

The storm really hit a few minutes later. The power went out and we lit candles. Anna went back into her room for some reason, and Adam and I were left alone in the kitchen, the candles giving everything a golden glow. He might look like a guy who lived in Brooklyn, but he was still handsome. When we first got together, we took pictures in this same room, the optimistic look of love on our faces, before things grew static, before the long stretches when he wouldn't answer his phone, before we couldn't stop yelling at each other.

We went back into the bedroom, previously ours and now just mine, and the taste of his mouth was so good while I kissed him that I started to regret everything, started to wonder if there was a way to fix it. But then I remembered the earring I'd found in the bed, right where my head was lying now. I'd only left the house to go to work that day. That's a sex-positive feminist for you. I kept kissing him anyway, and I loved the way his body felt over mine, his strong arms, his smooth skin, the animal stupidity of attraction. The sex with him was better in the beginning, better now that it was the end.

We got dressed. The power went back on but the internet stayed out. The three of us played cards at the kitchen table, and Anna and Adam drank beer while I watched. We turned on a DVD and Anna fell asleep. The movie ended. I looked out the window. It seemed like the rain and wind had stopped. I couldn't see much, just the light from the fat moon, a dull bulb blotted out by clouds.

It was late now but I was wide awake. Adam felt the same. Neither of us had anything to do the next day, the city still under a state of emergency. We decided to go out, see the damage.

"Should we wake up Anna?" Adam said.

I looked at him. This seemed insane. "What?" I said.

"It just seems, like, important," he said. "To see this."

Late last year, Adam was going to Occupy Wall Street every day with one of his bands, playing on a marching drum. He didn't have a job, the stereotype of drummers.

I had joined him when I could, when I wasn't in class or at one of my part-time jobs. Anna worked Monday through Friday in finance, was gone from early in the morning until late at night. On the weekends, she caught up on her sleep, did things like go on trips. One Saturday, Adam tried to make Anna join us. She refused. He got mad. "I don't want to go stand around a crowd of people on my day off," she had finally said.

Adam said some vague things about income inequality, this was a real movement for change, how she was on the wrong side of history if she didn't protest. I knew that Anna sent most of each paycheck home to her family, her mother sick with Parkinson's, two siblings still in elementary school.

Anna was quiet, measuring her thoughts. "I agree with them," she said. "I just don't see why it matters if I go."

I could tell that Adam kind of lost his mind at that point, but he pretended to not be upset, one more thing I hated about him. Instead, he calmly recited canned numbers and statistics, parameters of arguments made by someone else. I understood his point, but I had understood Anna's point too. She worked sixty hours a week. We didn't.

"I think we should let Anna sleep," I said. "We can go on our bikes. The two of us." I smiled at him, like I had an idea for a romantic date.

We headed to the park first. The streets were wet and dark, empty of everything but trash. A tree had crashed into the bus stop. A tree had crashed through a fence. A tree had crashed on the underpass of the BQE. A billboard had been ripped off, crumpled below on the sidewalk, a barely discernable message about Jesus. The awning had blown off the Dunkin' Donuts, broken plastic in the street, some splintered plywood, obstacles for our bikes.

We got to the park. The stadium lights were on for some reason, except for one that had crashed over, a tangle of metal and wood and wires. I took out my camera, snapped a picture, the dull lights reflecting off the wet grass. I tried to take one of Adam, silhouetted and leaning against his bike, but he protested. I quickly understood he didn't want me to take it because he was worried I would post it on Facebook, ruin his chances for whatever girl he was talking to who wasn't me. My heart was still pounding from the ride but also from the knowledge that this was a person fading, someone who was there in my life but also wasn't. Soon he would move out. Soon we would have another argument, inevitable, and soon it would become clear that stretching this whole thing out, our relationship, wasn't worth it. I set my bike down on the cement, lit a cigarette. Adam did the same. No need to lock up the bikes.

We walked around for a while, not talking, ripped-off branches, broken fences, spilled trash cans. I took more pictures, clicks of the mild apocalypse of a city. We started talking again, the book I was reading and a band that had opened up for his in Baltimore, they were good. Then Adam mentioned he wasn't voting for Obama in the primary, logic about drone strikes and bank bailouts. I'd never heard of the person he said he was voting for. I had some thoughts, a desire to tell him he was stupid. But what did it matter? He wasn't mine anymore.

We finished our cigarettes, got back on our bikes, decided to ride down to the water. We rode past the bank. Inside, the lights were on, and I could see a bunch of cops, milling around, doing nothing. I waited for Adam to say something about them but he didn't. We kept going, arrived at the pier.

Across the water, we could see Manhattan. It was black and empty, a massive power outage, and it felt like nothing was there, not a city but a negative space. On the ground, there was a perfectly intact three-foot sub, ham and swiss folded neatly between bread, as though there hadn't been a storm at all. I bent over, stuck my finger in the bread. It was wet. I ripped a piece off, the meat and cheese slimy, holding it out to Adam.

MATH CLASS

I was sitting on my bed, doing homework. It was late. I wasn't tired. I had the music on and maybe it was a little loud. Besides that, I wasn't doing anything wrong.

But then my roommate Greg flew into my room. He was yelling. For some reason my bedroom door had a glass window in it, like an office door, and he hit it against the wall so hard that it rattled. He wasn't making a lot of sense. I was a selfish bitch, I was out of control, blah blah blah. He pointed at the CD case on my desk, the chalky streak of Adderall, the empty vodka bottle. "Some people have to *wake up* at *five* in the *morning*," he screamed.

"Uhhhhhh," I said. "Do you want me to put on headphones?"

This made him shut up for a second, but then he went back to yelling. He got right up in my face and I could smell him, something sour. I wasn't that afraid, because he was a tiny little man, pale and doughy from sitting in front of screens. He had no friends, just his stupid job that he seemed to think was so damn important.

Then he said he'd have me killed. "I'll put your body in

a shallow grave on the side of the Fifteen," he said. I had to admit, the specificity of the exact freeway was a little unnerving. "You know I know people," he said, teeth gritted like he was in some gangster movie.

I didn't know if he knew people, not for sure, only certain that his father was in prison. Greg had told me it was because he was a hit man, but I didn't believe him. The truth was probably something dull, like tax evasion.

I laughed in his face. "Yeah, okay, go ahead. Murder me. Sounds good."

But then I sat there for a second, thinking about it, the fact that this little bitch man was threatening me in my own home. I was just doing my homework. The old feeling overtook me, that red wash of rage.

I'd done laundry earlier that day. There was a jumbo bottle of detergent by my bed. I picked it up. I have terrible aim. The bottle hit the office-door window, cleanly smashing through the glass, shards on the floor. I don't remember much from that point on but I must have tried to punch him because somehow I cut my wrist, a clean red line that later puffed into a white scar.

In the morning, my sheets were streaked with glass and blood, an ooze of Tide on the floor. I got up, drank coffee, made phone calls. I'd moved all my stuff into my mom's garage by the time Greg got off work. There wasn't much, just my bed and some boxes. It had been tense in the apartment for a while. A great excuse for a fresh start.

A week later, a friend with a truck helped me move into

my new apartment. A shabby little studio in a bad neighborhood, but it was my own. Greg hadn't contacted me, not even for the missing rent. Maybe he felt guilty. The building was old but charming. Crown moldings, claw-foot bathtub. Only a couple blocks from my community college. Not bad.

I'd been in remedial math for what felt like forty-six semesters. I wasn't stupid, just dropped out in tenth grade and got my GED instead. The people in my class were the same as me, mostly: not dumb but old or foreign or didn't pay attention in high school, failing the placement test due to a simple lack of vocabulary. So much math, and still nobody had told me what a cosine was. But I liked this semester so far. The teacher was nice and good at explaining things. I liked the homework, the graph paper and the calculator, the orderliness of the numbers falling into place, the fact that there was always one single right answer.

After we finished with the boxes, we were hungry. I'd seen a Mexican place on the corner, so we went there. Turned out to be in a little strip mall—a laundromat, a liquor store, a bar. Convenient. I was liking my new place more and more. We got burritos and they were good. It was early but we'd worked hard, so we decided to get a drink.

The bar was dark, just the pale swath of light from the door. My eyes adjusted and I saw cheesy flames and skulls painted across the wall. There were only a couple people in there, crusty bikers. But the bartender was my age, a sexy girl in cutoffs, and when we ordered vodka sodas they came in tall glasses, cheap, mostly vodka. Her name was Natasha. The second round, she didn't make us pay. I didn't remember walking home.

I got used to my new apartment, the sound of sirens at night and airplanes during the day. I did my homework. I made friends with the other people at the bar. I went nights, weekends, after class and work. The crowd didn't make sense: teachers, punks, drug dealers, lawyers. The only thing we seemed to have in common was we liked the cheap drinks and the dim light. Strangely, the people I started hanging out with the most was this couple, Richard and Joanna, a decade or two older than me. They seemed real normal—he was a doctor and she was a nurse, and if they weren't in scrubs they wore things like polo shirts and crisp jeans. But they were real funny and real smart, could put down the tall stiff drinks like water. Sometimes Joanna helped me with my homework at the bar, still remembering the formulas.

One Sunday, we were playing foosball, the three of us and some banker. I'd lived in the new place for six weeks by then, still hadn't heard a peep from stupid Greg. I was drinking a lot, too much, but I'd upped my Adderall consumption in turn and still had an A in math. The banker went to the bathroom, and Joanna asked if I partied. I wasn't sure what she meant. If *party* meant a threesome, then no, I didn't. I played dumb until she held out a little white bag in her palm.

"Oh," I said. "Yeah. I like to party."

We left the bar before the banker got back from the bathroom.

It wasn't until Richard had the lines railed out on my coffee table that I realized it was meth and not coke. I felt a little alarmed. One, because you can do coke and still be normal, but that's just not possible with meth. Two, I'd sworn I'd never do meth, having watched it turn various friends and acquaintances into pockmarked losers. But here they were, sitting on my futon, the drugs all laid out and just waiting to be done. It seemed too late to say no.

It burned, not just in my nose but in my whole face, tears filling my eyes. I remembered what I'd heard about meth, all the things it was cut with, ammonia and Drano. But a second later it kicked in, a whopping rush to my brain and my heart, like someone had shot me full of sunshine. I felt so good that I didn't give a shit about poison anymore. I wanted another line.

Richard and Joanna stayed over until dawn. All night, we did more lines, drank beer, smoked, listened to music, laughed, danced. It was a great night. They left me with the last bit of the drugs, a tiny pinch in a tiny baggy.

I woke up the next afternoon, alarm blaring. No time to fix my hair or put on makeup before class. My whole body ached, toes to teeth. I made coffee. My jaw felt swollen, the sides of my tongue scraped raw. The coffee turned my stomach. I drank it anyway, checking my calendar for today's homework assignment, because of course I hadn't thought to do that last night. Today's entry was blank. An overwhelming rush of unspecified dread, the chemical reaction to being high out of my mind. All I wanted was to get back in bed. But I reminded myself what a fuckup I was, twenty-three years old, a dumb druggie stuck in remedial math, and I needed to quit being a fuckup, so I pulled on a sweater and jeans and pushed myself out the door.

There was a homeless encampment on the walk to school. Sometimes I gave somebody a dollar when I had one and when they asked, but that day they ignored me like I was invisible, stared right through me from their tarps and sleeping bags. A swell of nausea. I vomited into the bushes by the freeway entrance, splashing my shoes. The vomit was bile and coffee, liquid and brownish yellow. It left an almost-citrus sting on my tongue.

At school, I went to the bathroom, rinsed out my mouth, wiped off my shoes. There I was, pretending to be normal, an A student, ready for class. I checked my phone. I still miraculously had fifteen minutes before class. I took a deep breath right before I walked into the classroom, reminded myself this would all be over in about an hour. I sat in my chair, pulled out my book and my pencils and paper. But then I saw the words on the whiteboard:

ONLY PENCILS ON DESK BEFORE EXAM

Oh shit, I thought. Shit, oh shit, oh shit. I had completely forgotten about the midterm, like a complete fucking meth-snorting fuckup.

But then I remembered I had that tiny baggy.

I still had time. I went to the bathroom, railed tiny lines on my compact. It was a delicate operation, trying to not tilt the mirror or make noise while I chopped. I flushed the toilet right before I snorted it, but my timing was off and the girl in the next stall probably knew exactly what I was up to.

I had so much fun taking that midterm, the neat logic of the numbers and letters, even the scratchy sound of all our pencils marking at once. My brain was firing so fast and so sharp that I finished in twenty minutes. I double-checked my answers and they all seemed good, and still not even half the allotted time had passed. I turned in my test anyway, sailed out the door. The school was in the middle of downtown, our class at the top of a four-story building that overlooked a courtyard, a hollow square. You could see the bay and the airport and the sunny sloping hills, the edge of green that made up the golf course. The sun was going down and the light was that soft fuzzy color. I felt fucking great.

But that night, in bed, still not able to sleep, it occurred to me that the meth hadn't made me smart but stupid. That the questions I thought I'd gotten right were probably all wrong. That there was no way I could have finished that test in twenty minutes. I'd probably missed an entire page. I tried to calculate my grade with an A in the homework and quizzes but an F on the midterm. Probably a C. All that hard work down the drain.

On Wednesday, I took a shot to ease the pain of the F before I went to class. I had a killer hangover from the night before, head pounding and that cloaking feeling of doom. When I got to the fourth floor, everyone was standing around outside, staring down into the courtyard like a bunch of fools. One of them was talking loud and fast into her cell phone, some language I couldn't identify. I walked into the classroom but it was empty. I checked the time. Maybe I was early. But it was ten minutes till, same as always. I got my homework out of my backpack, checked my answers.

My teacher finally walked into the room and right away I could tell something was wrong. She was always so calm and so happy-seeming, but that day her face was all twisted up, neat hair out of place, and it seemed like she was short of breath.

"Claire," she said at me, like she was surprised I was even there.

"Hi," I said, feeling nervous.

She said nothing, opened her mouth, closed it. Her hands were shaking. "There's been an accident," she finally said. A dead husband, maybe. The reason why the others were outside. "You can pick up your test and go home."

She shuffled through the stack of papers on the desk, red letter grades on the corners, Cs and Fs. She had to go through it a couple times before she found mine, eyes down like it was terrible to look at me, or maybe it was just terrible to look at anyone. I felt sorry for her, for whatever her accident was. I wondered if a hug was appropriate, decided against it; I probably smelled like alcohol anyway. Finally she found my test, handed it to me with a tight little smile, I couldn't tell whether it was congratulatory or conciliatory. She still hadn't looked me in the eye.

I put the test in my backpack without looking at it. "Do you want the homework?" I asked.

She was writing something on the whiteboard. My question made her jump. "Oh, no," she said. "I'll just get it next class."

I looked at what she'd written.

COUNSELOR: BRIDGET FRANK
ROOM F12
619-555-6212

"If you need to talk to someone," she said, pointing.

I felt my face turn red, my stomach swelling with sick. I was a mess, a dumb druggie fuckup. It was obvious. I looked down at the ground while I walked out.

Everyone was still standing around, still looking at the courtyard. I tapped this woman on the shoulder, a mom I always talked to after class, named Cindy or Mindy or maybe Mandy. "What happened?"

She turned to me, her brown eyes flat as glass but then her lip quivered. "Jonah jumped off the math building. Just a bit ago. He's dead."

"This building?"

"Yes," she said.

"Down there?"

"Yes."

Some of the others had turned around, were now staring at me. All of them were clearly upset: the guy old enough to be a grandfather, the girl from Russia, these twins who were both dumb as rocks.

"Who's Jonah?" I asked.

"Oh my god," she said, hugging herself.

It all seemed a little overdramatic but I patted her on the shoulder anyway. "But who's Jonah?" I asked again.

She pulled away from me. "*Jonah*," she said, like I was stupid. "From our class. He sat right next to you."

I tried to picture the person who sat next to me but it was blank. Jonah. The name meant nothing. "Oh god," I said. "That's terrible." I wrinkled my face appropriately for the occasion.

"He was so *nice*," Cindy or Mindy said. People always pull this shit in a tragedy, acting like the sad thing belongs only to them. I wondered if she'd ever even talked to him.

But I pretended too, pretended I knew who this Jonah was and that I thought he was nice. "It's so sad," I said.

I wondered what was down there, how far things had progressed. Brains, blood, broken bones, a gurney. I didn't want to know. The grandpa was looking over the railing again; the twins were holding each other by the arms. I wondered if there was something wrong with me, or with them, that I had no desire to look. I couldn't figure out why everyone was still standing there.

There was nothing more for me to do or say. I took the

elevator so I couldn't accidentally look over the stairs. I walked the couple blocks to the bar, smoking a cigarette. I thought about my math test, the F, the dead kid, if there would be a stain on the concrete the next time I went to class.

When I got to the bar, I ordered another shot and a drink. "Some guy killed himself," I told Natasha. "Jumped off the math building."

"Oh shit," Natasha said. "Did you know him?"

"No," I said. I didn't. I wondered if he'd really sat next to me, how I'd missed that. "It was only four stories."

"Damn," she said. "I didn't know you could die from that."

"I didn't either," I said. "At least we got out early."

She laughed, turned to pour somebody else a beer. I downed the shot, opened my backpack. When I felt the warmth in my bones, I pulled out the test. I'd gotten an A. Ninety-eight percent. Almost perfect.

I AM THE SNAKE

My mom picked me up at the airport. The trip was half-emergency, half-planned. She'd gotten there three days earlier than our original tickets, but I arrived on time.

I always forgot that summertime in Baltimore was hot and wet. The air hit me thick when I walked out of the airport. I stood on the curb, the cement radiating and sweat popping on my lip. My mom pulled up in the rental car, air-conditioning blasting. I settled in the seat and wiped a tear of sweat from between my thighs.

"Your uncle's house," she said, and then she paused. "It's a mess."

This was the emergency part. My cousin Heather, Uncle Leo's daughter, had arrived a week earlier, our annual family trip to Baltimore, wanting to spend time with her father. But Leo kept falling asleep. In the middle of the night, she saw strange people coming into and out of the apartment in the basement. Leo left one day to go to the "grocery store," and Heather looked under the mattress and found a needle. I didn't know that could happen—a sixty-something man suddenly becoming a junkie. Heather called Leo's sisters, my mom and Aunt Becky. That was when my mom changed her tickets to fly out early. They were trying to find my uncle a rehab.

We pulled up to the house, a white clapboard on a tree-lined street, the house the family had moved into after my grandfather died. We walked into the kitchen, and it looked the same as always, the same oak cabinets and blue walls, dark in the middle of the day. I hugged Heather and she looked tired. Uncle Leo was "resting" in his bedroom.

My mom poured me a glass of water, and then we walked down the stairs. "I was cleaning up the basement," she said. The house had scared me when I was little because it was dark and felt like a tower. Three narrow floors, not including the attic or my grandma's basement apartment, connected by a single staircase. In the old days, back when everyone except my mom still lived in Baltimore, we spent most of the day with my aunt and cousin Nicholas in Grandma Thea's apartment. In the evenings, we came up to Leo's, and the grown-ups sat around the tiny kitchen table, laughing and drinking and smoking cigarettes. My mom didn't normally smoke. They all had thick Baltimore accents, except my mother who had scrubbed hers clean when she moved to California. In Baltimore, it came back, my mother speaking like the person she'd been before she was my mother. They talked so loud together, the abrasive accent, the sharp twisted r's, smoking and drinking. It all made me dizzy, like somebody else's family, not mine.

The basement apartment was the mess.

"Jesus," I said.

There was only one couch down there, no other furniture, no appliances. The cushions on the couch were missing. On the floor were cigarette butts, weird stains, beer and energy drink cans, empty pizza boxes, tiny ziplock bags, the drug kind. Crumpled balls of aluminum foil. There were black trash bags piled in the corner. "We had to call the police to kick some people out," my mom said. "Some of Leo's *friends*. Guess they were basically living in the basement."

I knew what that meant. The old apartment had transformed from a granny flat into a trap house. That was how I was going to spend my afternoon. Cleaning up a trap house. There was no air-conditioning and we were both already sweating.

"Here," my mom said, handing me a new pair of leather work gloves. "Watch out for needles. We've found three. It looks a lot better than it did."

"Shouldn't we get, like, professional cleaners?" I said.

"Too expensive," my mom said, and then she turned on a loud box fan in the corner.

I ripped the tags off the gloves and then I helped my mom clean up, delicately picking up cans and throwing them in a trash bag. I didn't find any needles, just spoons, the plastic bags.

◆

That night I couldn't sleep. We were staying at my aunt's condo. When she got divorced from my cousin Nicholas's father, they sold the big house they'd had in the woods, and with the money she bought a house in Florida, where she lived most of the year, and a tiny two-bedroom condo for when she was visiting Nicholas in Baltimore. The old house had been beautiful, big glass windows overlooking trees, lots of bedrooms, a pool. Here, I slept on the couch. My mom was asleep in the spare room.

I got up from the sofa bed, using my phone as a flashlight to open the front door. The condo complex was dark and quiet. I walked down the narrow paths until I found a patch of grass near some trees. I sat and smelled the green and wet, lit a cigarette. It smelled so different here than it did in California. The crickets were buzzing loudly in the bushes like a wall, fireflies in the air. To me, fireflies were a piece of my child-hood: exclusive to Baltimore. The paths of the condo complex were lit up by lights, marking the sidewalks, and there were no fireflies on them but the trees and the bushes were black silhouettes. The fireflies flew up and down that blackness, like they were self-contained under glass. One landed on my bare thigh, blinking green once before flying away.

◆

The next day, we were sitting in a parking lot in the rental car. Aunt Becky reached into her purse, gold bracelets jangling from her wrist, and pulled out a small tub of Vicks. "Here," she said. "Put this under your nose. It stinks in there." I had a vase of flowers between my feet. We passed the tub around, my mother, my cousin Nicholas, me, and my aunt Becky, rubbing a dot on our upper lip. It smudged Becky's pink lipstick. I picked up the vase of flowers and we buzzed the button into the nursing home.

"Hi, Carol," Nicholas said to the woman at the front desk. "Oh, hey, Nicholas," Carol said back. Nicholas was the only good one. He came once, twice, a week, lived nearby because he worked at a museum in DC. The rest of us saw Thea once, twice a year.

The nursing home smelled like disinfectant but also like piss, shit, and vomit. The Vicks only partially worked, mostly just adding one more smell. We walked down the corridor, and the nursing home was so ugly, everything dingy, the floors, the walls. The doors to the rooms were open, and most of the old people were in their beds, looking up at us as we walked by. *Is that a person for me?* their faces said. An old woman, nearly skeletonized, with wild white hair, opened her mouth at me, the pink circle of her throat. I could have been one of her grandchildren, but I wasn't.

Grandma Thea was wearing a flowered nightgown thing, sitting in bed, a yellow blanket on her lap. Her white hair was freshly curled. Nicholas had taken her to the beauty parlor the day before.

Nicholas sat down on the edge of the bed. The rest of us stood over her. Grandma smiled at us. She'd been mostly happy since they put her on Prozac, Nicholas said, like she wasn't in the room. Everybody in my family took Prozac, it seemed, except for me. I took a mood stabilizer.

The last time I'd seen Thea was the year before, right after she moved out of the old house. When my grandfather died, before I was born, he'd left my grandmother near penniless. Uncle Leo stepped in, only twenty-one years old, buying that house so everyone could live there. Then my grandmother developed dementia and moved to the nursing home.

The basement apartment of my childhood was my grandma with the TV on, soap operas and talk shows, and we'd sit around and I'd look at all her catalogs and all her *Reader's Digests*. My Christmas and birthday presents came from those catalogs, a teddy bear I still slept with sometimes. She tried to make us eat. There were stale cookies in tins and Ritz crackers and Entenmann's cakes and macaroni salad in plastic tubs from the grocery store. "You hungry? I got some crackers. You want some cookies?" The refrain of immigrant grandmothers. That was when I first noticed the dementia. She asked me if I wanted the same crackers three times in an hour. I was a decade younger than the other cousins, and even though I was older than Uncle Leo had been when he bought the house, they still treated me like a child. It left me quiet, no opinions, nothing to say, and when Grandma brought me the crackers, I had to eat them, three times. That was the same visit as the tampons. A commercial for Tampax played on TV and suddenly my grandma turned to me. "Never put anything in your vagina," she said firmly, and we all sat there, trying to keep straight expressions, but then my aunt laughed straight in her face.

"You've got your babies," Nicholas said. My mom took the flowers from me, set the vase on a table.

"Yes," Thea said. She was holding two cheap-looking baby dolls in her lap, blond hair painted on their heads, wearing pink rompers. "Bonnie and Becky."

"Look at her baby dolls," Nicholas said. He was laughing. That's what my family did. They laughed at everything. "It's Bonnie and Becky. And who are these people?" Nicholas pointed to us.

Grandma Thea stared. She looked confused. "Bonnie and Becky," she said.

"Right!" my mom said. She touched her hand. All of our hands looked the same, small palms, long fingers. My mother's and my aunt's had age freckles. My grandmother's skin was thin, and you could see her veins. "And who is this?" my mom said, pointing to me. But Thea didn't remember. I was nobody to her, a stranger.

◆

That evening, we went back to the old house and Leo was in the kitchen, drinking coffee and sweating. My mom told me to take him to an AA meeting. I'd been going myself for five years, had the bronze coin I got on my anniversary in my wallet. I pulled the list of meetings up on my laptop. I didn't know how to find a good one in this city, so I just chose the closest.

My uncle drove in his old Cadillac and classic rock played

on the stereo. I didn't know how I was supposed to treat him, like my uncle or like anyone else in recovery. He was quiet. I realized I knew almost nothing about him, just the basic details related to our family. Two daughters. A dead wife. That he bought the house, lived there for forty years. I didn't know what his job had been, if he was retired now, how he got along with my mother, how he'd fallen into heroin. I wanted to ask him but it seemed too weird, this person I'd known my whole life, making the equivalent of small talk. We both sat anxiously in the sound of the radio, waiting for one of us to have something to say. "How are you feeling?" I finally asked him.

In AA, if you asked someone how they were feeling, you usually got an honest answer. But all he said was, "Eh, I think I'm doing okay," and then we went back to silence.

The meeting was at an old Methodist church but in a newer building off to the side that was plain. The room looked like it was used for the kids' Bible study when it wasn't used for meetings, crayon pictures of Christ tacked on a bulletin board. We got tiny cups of Styrofoam coffee, the comfort of all meetings being mostly the same, the smell of church, the big metal coffeepot, the powdered creamer. Somebody had brought cookies from the grocery store, sugar with pink crystal sprinkles, and I wanted to tell Leo that he should eat some but I didn't. We sat down on the cold metal chairs in the last row. I read the backs of the chairs in front of me. The name of the church was stamped on them but *Methodist* was abbreviated: ST PETERS METH CHURCH.

The meeting was the kind that was filled with old men, old-timers. The old men drank their coffee and told their stories, car wrecks and getting kicked out of bars. When they asked for newcomers and visitors, I raised my hand, Emily, an alcoholic visiting from San Diego. I wondered if Leo would say anything, and I thought he wasn't going to but then he did. He stood up, Leo, an alcoholic, and then he walked toward the front, took the silver twenty-four-hour coin, and I watched him flush red as the old man shook his hand. When he sat back down, he held the coin lightly between his fingers but then he placed it in his palm, holding it in a closed fist until the meeting ended.

We smoked cigarettes on the steps with the old men, and Leo was laughing and pretending everything was fine. They were giving him slips of paper with their phone numbers. One of the old men told him the thing about sugar, handed him a cookie. Then the leaves in the trees started shaking and the sky turned yellow. The storm hit on the way home, sheets on the windshield. But Leo stopped at the 7-Eleven anyway, came back with a fistful of candy bars. He held the steering wheel with one hand as he ate a Baby Ruth with the other, licking melted chocolate off his thumbs.

We got stuck at a red light, everyone driving slow because of the rain, so heavy it was hard to see the road. I wanted to talk to Leo, treat him like a regular addict.

"My problem was pills," I said. "I don't know if my mom told you that." And then I told him that when I'd lived in New York and was newly sober, I'd feel so awful and then

I'd walk down to the bodega, buy a fancy five-dollar chocolate bar and eat the whole thing. All AA meetings shared
the same wisdom. In the early days of sobriety, it is sugar,
meetings, phone calls, repeated clichés, this strange idea
of a higher power—they're all treated as magical currency
that could keep you sober, and you listen, pretend, because
there is nothing else you can do. I remembered, right out of
rehab, my sponsor taking me down to the waterfront, the
river glossy and black, her telling me to kneel and pray. I
never prayed, I didn't even know what I was praying to, but
I did it anyway and I felt crazy, talking to nothing, but when
I stood up again, something small and heavy in me lifted.
Leo and I ran into the house, both of us getting soaked in
the rain, the sky growling thunder.

♦

We were taking Thea to dinner. The nurse had put her in
some sort of tunic, slightly nicer than a nightgown, fas-
tened an old gold chain around her neck. We wheeled her
out of the nursing home, past the other old people and their
old-people smells with their open doors, craning their necks
to stare at her jealously. Thea smiled the whole time. I wasn't
even sure she knew what was happening.

I sat in the back of the car with Thea, hands folded in
her lap, looking out the window, and something about her
reminded me of a little girl, the idle blankness in her face.

We used to go to this restaurant every year, with the other

cousins, with my uncle and dad before the divorces, with the great-aunts and great-uncles before the deaths. We used to make reservations for the private room because there were so many of us. Now we just ate at a regular table. Nicholas tucked the plastic bib onto Thea like she was a baby, but then the rest of us tucked bibs on ourselves too. They dumped the bucket of crabs on the table. When I was little the crabs freaked me out and I just ate chicken nuggets from a plate. Now I ate the crabs off the brown paper. I was terrible at opening them, mashing the meat with my cracker. My mom finally grabbed it from me, did it herself. "Here," she said, handing me a crab with its breastplate pulled away. There was yellow paste in its guts, and I tried not to think about what it was, digestive enzymes, and pretend it was what my family called it, mustard.

I picked out the meat with my fingers, watching my grandma crack her crabs. She didn't know who I was, but she was able to delicately crack their claws as though it were nothing, pull the flesh clean away with her teeth.

◆

We were sitting upstairs in Leo's house. The basement was mostly clean, all the trash gone. They'd found Leo a rehab, and he and Heather were packing his bags upstairs.

I had woken up that morning feeling bad. It still happened sometimes, despite all the step work and the therapy and medication. Everything was slightly off, like I was looking at the world crooked. They were sending me out for sandwiches, one last lunch before Leo left. I wasn't hungry, and everybody kept changing their mind about what they wanted. I'd write something down and then I'd scribble it out, write something else.

"Oh, and we should get some Coke for Emmie," my aunt said, using the name they called me when I was a little girl, which I had asked to not be called anymore when I was six years old. I wanted to be called my full name, Emily. I didn't want to be told what to buy for myself. I didn't even drink Coke. All I drank was coffee and water. I didn't write down the Coke.

When they'd finally made up their minds, Becky looked over the list. "You forgot the Coke," she told me. I didn't say anything. She took the pen from my hand and added *Coke* in her perfect cursive at the bottom.

There was pointless traffic on the streets. I hit all the red lights. It was hot and it took forever for the air conditioner to kick on. I turned on the radio but I didn't know any of the stations and every channel I came across was either bad or static. When I finally got to the parking lot, everyone was just sitting there, stupid idiots in giant SUVs, and I couldn't turn into a parking space, blinker blinking pointlessly. I felt a flash of suicide, the old feeling I got where I wanted to die, even though I didn't want to die. I imagined myself gunning it, crashing into the big SUV that was preventing me from turning. I knew these thoughts weren't real, they were just intrusive things that popped into my head, but they still wormed their way in. Whenever it happened, I tried to counter it, remind myself that I actually wanted to be alive, a tip from an old therapist. "I love being alive," I growled, slamming my palms against the steering wheel. And then the SUV moved and I parked the car. I walked into the grocery store, pushed the thought of slashing my wrists away. "I love being alive," I whispered.

I got the sandwiches and the Coke. The guy who made the sandwiches was nice, smiled at me, gave me a free cookie. When I got back to the house, my aunt handed me a glass of ice, poured the Coke in it, bubbles foaming and crackling. I took a sip. It was cold and it was sweet and the bubbles felt so nice on my throat.

Everyone sat down at the table but there wasn't enough room for me so I stood at the counter. I watched Leo as he ate his sandwich. He didn't eat much, didn't participate in the conversation. I remembered when I went to rehab. I remembered the queasy stomach, a feral feeling like an animal. After five years of recovery I'd seen so many people relapse, so many people die. I hoped it would stick for Leo. I said a little prayer for him, chewing on my turkey sandwich, talking in my head to something I still wasn't entirely sure I believed in. *God, please keep him sober. Please give him strength. Please.*

◆

Leo was in rehab and we were flying home the next morning. We were back at the nursing home, saying goodbye to Grandma Thea. I didn't know it would be the last time I'd see her alive. I still felt mentally ill, and that day all the lonely old people made me want to cry, a bare mattress because somebody had died. We walked into her room and my mom went to change the water in the vase of flowers. I sat down in the chair next to her bed. "Hi, Grandma," I said, and reached for her hands. She pulled them away, her eyes beady in terror, gasping. "Who is that?" she said. "Why is it at my bed?"

My mom laughed. "That's Emmie, your granddaughter," she said.

"My granddaughter," Grandma repeated, looking at me suspiciously. "We're related."

"Yes," I said. "I'm Bonnie's daughter."

She looked at the baby dolls in her lap, and then she looked at my mother.

"Its eyes are green," Grandma said.

"Yes," I said. Everybody else's were brown, the Greek.

"You look like . . ." she said, searching, "a snake. You're a snake. Get away from me!"

I stood up from the chair. I knew she was being silly, an old woman who didn't know what she was saying. But something in me felt like she was seeing me, who I was. The snake coiled inside of me, resting.

RATIONAL FEARS FOR ONLY CHILDREN

True Ghost Stories

At the bookstore I picked out this book called *True Ghost Stories*. My dad bought it for me, no questions asked, even though I got nightmares from just about everything, including *The Care Bears Movie* and a computer game about dinosaurs. I only made it through the first story. It was about a woman who lived in a haunted house. Every night, she woke up at the same time—3:33—and there would be a ghost sleeping next to her. She could feel the weight of it, the way its mass caused the mattress to slope. Sometimes it would stroke her hair, rub her back, with its icy ghost fingers.

Late at night there were times I felt a ghost slip into my bed, pressing down on the mattress and shooting the room with cold. Sometimes I felt it tracing the line of my spine. I always closed my eyes tight and tried to remember that ghosts weren't real, but I never fell for it, so instead I'd chant, "Go away, go away, go away," over and over until I finally fell asleep.

The Boogeyman

Sometimes when I was bad, my parents told me that I'd better shape up or the boogeyman would get me. I pictured a giant man-shaped snot pile running around. I didn't want to get slimed and thought it sounded gross, but I didn't understand how it was supposed to be scary enough to get me to behave.

Then at some point I realized they were saying *boogeyman*, not *booger man*. They told me he lived under my bed. I checked under there a few times and all I saw was dust. But then I watched a movie at a friend's house called *Little Monsters*. It starred Fred Savage, who found a man with blue skin and horns living under his bed. A boogeyman.

Sometimes at night I heard things move, saw shadows in the closet, swore there was something growling under my bed. He'd wrap his blue hands around my throat and hold them there and he'd force me to kiss him, sucking out my breath with his mouth.

Amoebas

We were in the northern part of Ohio one summer, camping on a lake, and my dad thought it was a good idea to tell me about amoebas. They are single-celled organisms, more a blob than an insect or animal. Most of the time they are harmless, but there is a chance that they could crawl up your nose, make their way into your brain, and kill you. They don't exist in the ocean, only in water that is warm and still.

My dad told me this when he saw me dunking my head in the water. "Let me know if you get a headache," he said, and then he laughed. I ran out of the water screaming, and he felt bad and chased after me, hugging me as I cried, telling me they were very, very rare, unlikely to be found in this type of water. But it was too late. For years I was terrified of still water—lakes, swimming pools, even puddles. Something that had once been benign was now deadly, a threat.

The House Burning Down

At school we had some firemen come in to teach us fire safety. They were big and muscly and one of them had very hairy arms. They told us about "stop, drop, and roll." They told us not to play with matches, to never touch a hot oven, to make sure each floor and each bedroom had a working smoke alarm. Then they said every family needs a fire plan, complete with a map and safe spot. At the end of the presentation, they gave us each a plastic fire hat and a coloring book that doubled as an informative pamphlet.

I took my pamphlet home and showed it to my parents at dinner. They laughed at me for being so serious, but then they took me through the house, me on my dad's shoulders so I could press the TEST button on each of our smoke alarms.

Then we got out the graph paper and markers. Mom drew an outline of our house, the different rooms and windows and doors. We drew arrows pointing out the primary escape route for each room in red, the secondary in yellow. But when it came time to decide on a safe place, she seemed to stop caring. "Can't it just be the street?" she said.

I explained that cars could run us over, but she said she didn't think it was a concern and got up to do something else. We didn't even get a chance to decide on the items we would save.

So that night, I thought it over. The photo albums. The music box that had once belonged to my great-grandmother. My stuffed Kitty. But what about the important papers, our banking information and birth certificates? I didn't even know where those were kept. I sat there thinking about our identities burning up, how after the fire we wouldn't even know who we were anymore. I wasn't sure, but it seemed like my parents could renounce me without my birth certificate. If that went up in flames, I'd always have to be on my best behavior.

Then I went over the ways I would get out of the house. I imagined the smoke alarm going off, touching my door, finding it hot. I imagined jumping out of my window, hitting the ground hard, knocking out my breath, but being okay. I imagined picking myself up and going in the street to find Mom and Dad. I imagined it empty. I imagined hearing their screams.

Strangers with Candy

There was a lot of talk about stranger danger and needles in Halloween candy. You weren't supposed to ever take candy from someone you didn't know. You were supposed to yell *no* and then run away. Sometimes I had nightmares of scary men asking me if I wanted some candy, me saying *no* and then running away—just like I was supposed to—but it didn't matter, they would catch me and shove the candy into my mouth, and it was full of needles and poison that made me vomit blood.

Every time I was alone and saw a van, I froze. I figured that this was it. There was a man in there, on the hunt for a little girl like me, just waiting to force-feed me poison candy. I never took the lollipops at the bank or doctor's. The scary part of Halloween wasn't the ghosts or haunted houses or masks. It was the candy, the treat.

Killer Swarms

I wasn't afraid of bugs in the usual way. Spiders weren't creepy to me; if I saw a daddy longlegs, I liked to pick it up and let it crawl over my arms. If there were crickets in the house, I didn't mind catching them with my hands or a glass to release them out the back door. When we had flies in the summer, I was the one who went around with the flyswatter, smacking them and listening to their bodies crunch.

But bees and ants were a different story. It was hard to walk in the desert without finding an ant nest, the holes they'd dug in the ground surrounded by piles of sand. Sometimes you wouldn't know you were standing on one until it was too late, until they were over your shoes and legs. And the news showed reports of killer bees, a new thing, they'd just recently migrated up from Mexico. If you walked too close, they would think you were threatening their hive and attack you.

I couldn't see one bee or one ant without seeing a swarm. Their bodies trying to crowd into my ears, eyes, mouth, and nose. Swallowing them, my organs punctured by stings and bites. Crawling underneath my clothes, so even if I ran away, the bugs went with me, the only way to escape them was to be someone else, to wait, to zip out of my own skin.

Getting Kidnapped by Goblins

I had a book about a girl who was taking care of her baby sister, and when she wasn't paying attention some goblins came in and took the baby away because they wanted her for their bride. In her place, they left a baby made of ice. The big sister had to go to the goblin world to get the baby back, and it took all night to rescue her.

Somehow I became convinced that if I read the book, it would summon the goblins and they would come and take me away. I didn't want to be a goblin bride. I didn't want to have to kiss or dance with goblins.

Because I had no brother or sister to come save me, I would just stay gone. My mom would come to wake me for school, but all she'd find would be a puddle of cold water where the ice version of me had melted, and by then the sun would have risen already and it would be much too late.

My Parents Dying Suddenly in Their Sleep

Every night, the last thing my parents said to me was "I love you," and every night, the last thing I said to them was "I love you too." One night I was really mad at them—we'd gotten into a fight because they wanted me to put away my toys before bed and I had said I would after I finished my TV show, but they misunderstood and thought I was ignoring them and it just turned into a big old mess, with them screaming and me crying. I put away my toys, still crying, and then I brushed my teeth and got into bed. Mom came in and told me "I love you," like usual, but I was still mad so I said nothing. She said "I love you" again, louder this time, and again I ignored her. "Okay, fine," she said, closing the door. "But what if I die in my sleep? You'll have to carry that for the rest of your life—that you refused to say you loved me."

I sat there for a moment. I hadn't known that could happen. I knew people could die, but I thought it was always because they were really sick or got murdered or something. I didn't know they could just up and die, a surprise. I ran into my parents' room and told them I loved them, oh how I loved them, and they said they loved me too and we smiled and hugged and I went back to my room.

I had a hard time getting to sleep, and when I finally did it was hard for me to stay that way. I kept thinking about my parents dying in their sleep, wondering how it felt to wake up an orphan. Finally, when it was very late, almost 4:00

a.m., I snuck into their room to make sure they were still alive. I opened their door, quietly as I could, walked slowly and silently to their bed. My dad was breathing deeply, in and out, his chest going up and down, definitely alive, but I wasn't so sure about my mom. I stuck my finger underneath her nose, to see if I could feel the air coming in and out. I did—it was soft and warm.

From then on, for years, I would wake up from night-mares and have to do the same thing. Sometimes they'd wake up, wondering what the hell I was doing there in their room, standing over them, my hands next to their faces. It seemed impossible to tell them the truth—just checking to make sure you're not dead.

Spontaneous Human Combustion

Images, grainy ones, of fragmented bodies sitting in charred furniture, legs ending in shoes like normal, but then, above the knee, an explosion of black rubble. I don't know where I saw them. Maybe *Unsolved Mysteries*. Wherever it was, it stuck with me.

When we had library time at school, I would sneak off to the aisle with the encyclopedias and look it up. One case told of a woman at a nightclub in England during the 1930s. It was New Year's. She had been dancing one minute, and the next she was engulfed in hot blue flame. No one saw the fire begin; no one could find its source. All they knew was she had burned in a flash, leaving behind only diamond earrings and a small pile of ash and bones. I pictured her dancing, twirling till her heart beat so fast it made heat against her chest, till the soles of her shoes smoked, till her hair glowed, till she caught on fire, till she was dead.

The books told me that some people believed it was psychokinesis—the mind did it to the body. Every time I got upset, I waited for it to happen to me. I could feel the fire starting, the embers in my chest feeding one another until I burst into flames.

HAZEL: A DIPTYCH

ADA (1985–)

My family never spoke about her. She died long before I was born. She had three children, including my father, each bringing her up as infrequently as possible. The ways they described her were never kind.

Everything I knew about my grandmother: Her name was Hazel. She was a decade older than my grandfather. They met in Los Angeles after the war. She came from Nebraska.

OCTOBER 2017

For the memorial of my aunt, Hazel's daughter, I got on a small plane and then a big plane and then I drove two

HAZEL (1916–1972)

I was born in the heat of summer, a sweltering day. A sparrow flew smack into the bedroom window when Mother was in labor, fell dead in the dirt. For years, she thought it was a bad omen. But then I went and turned out fine, as far as she knew. Smart. Pretty. Capable.

What she didn't know was all that I kept hidden. Secrets, regrets, a sense of thwarted ambition. All the unnamed feelings, vast and deep like the ocean.

hours to my cousin's house. When I got there, I remembered one more thing my father had told me about Hazel. During the holidays, she prepared multicourse meals, dozens of desserts, staying up for days, everything to excess, before collapsing in her bedroom, unmoving and mute, for twice as long. The reason he hates Christmas.

And now in the kitchen of my cousin, Hazel's granddaughter, I unwrapped the cheeses and meats, placed them on a platter; I arranged the cookies; I sliced the bread; I roughly filled a bowl of temporarily abandoned cream puffs, cutting them in half rather than punching a hole, to save time. So much food for a girl whose mother just died to take on. My cousin was mostly smiling, mostly unhurried, but in the still moments I watched something small in her crumble.

People were already arriv-
ing by the time I was arranging
old photos of my aunt above
a makeshift altar. This is the
type of family we are, the
type that remembers the dead
through memorials instead of
funerals. There were pictures
of my dead aunt, with her dead
brother, with her dead father,
with my father, my cousin, me,
all of her ex-husbands—but not
a single picture of Hazel. Her
mother.

More remembered facts:
Hazel was the oldest sister in a
large family. She was a nurse.
She saved bacon grease in coffee cans to cook with later, and
everything she made tasted
like rancid bacon. She beat
my father. She was bipolar,
undiagnosed, the genetic link
to my own mental illness, the
reason I am the way I am.

Right before I left, my
cousin handed me a bun-
dle made from an old lace

handkerchief. In it, jewelry belonging to my aunt: turquoise rings, a diamond-chip necklace. Also a little gold pin, Hazel's, that she had received when she graduated as a nurse.

We were standing next to my father, the three surviving Connollys. Same eyes, same compact body, same long, crooked fingers.

I held out the pin, showed it to my father. He turned it over in his hand, recognizing it immediately.

"She was so proud of this," he said. "So proud of being a nurse."

It was the first time I'd ever heard him say anything about her that was remotely kind.

Her initials were engraved in tiny script on the back: HC, Hazel Connolly. He was quiet for a moment, still. Then he said, "You know, it's funny, but I can't remember her name."

My cousin and I, her grand-daughters, born a decade after she died, reminded him. Hazel Connolly.

DECEMBER 1932

Christmas Eve, Mama baking rolls in the kitchen. Susie was supposed to be putting ribbons on the tree but really was just playing with her dolls. I was threading popcorn. The house was quiet for once, the boys all out, somewhere, and the only sounds were the fire and Susie babbling. For once, everything felt safe and warm.

But then the door flew open, Father all wet and covered with snow, a gust of storm and cold air. He bent down to take off his boots and he looked at me, so hard and so sharp I thought for sure that Mama would see. But nothing happened. He just took off his boots and went upstairs.

A bead of blood. I guess I had stuck myself, surprised by his look, so bare that

YOU ARE THE SNAKE

anyone could have read his
face. The pain felt good. I
sucked the blood.

That was what started it,
my latest bad habit. When
my body filled with the
sickness, the dark damp
feeling of death, I pricked
my finger. When Mama
was out and he pushed me
in the bathroom, afterward,
I pricked my finger. A valve,
a release, a little whoosh of
wind on a hot day.

For a while, that's all it
was. Soon, I wanted more.
I started pricking more
than once, the dots of blood
on my fingertip like a pox.
One time I poked so hard I
couldn't get the needle out,
had to yank it with my teeth,
wrap my finger in cloth, and
call it an accident. Another
time, I got the bright idea
to shove it under the bed of
my nail, the pain so sharp it
scraped my throat.

One day, I was upset for no reason I could name. It was springtime, the weather clear and fair, an A on my essay at school. There was nothing wrong, nothing at all, but still I was in such a foul mood, something nasty in me, hot and boiling. I pulled the needle out of the little cloth packet I now kept in my pocket. I jabbed it in my finger, watched the blood bloom. I did it again. I did it again. Ten little pricks, one for each body in this cursed house. But still I couldn't settle myself, couldn't flick myself out of it.

On the counter, a jar of pickles. The boys had just gotten home from school. They were always forgetting to put things back. I unscrewed the lid. I put my bloody finger right in that jar.

The vinegar stung in a way I can only describe as delicious. A delicious pain, enveloping my body so completely I was aware of nothing else, no thoughts in my silly head.

I didn't even notice that Donald was in the room. The boys were all mean but he was the meanest, sharp eyes and a sharper tongue.

"What are you doing?" he said.

My hand was still in the jar. I couldn't think of a good excuse so I just took it out, tried not to blush.

"Freak show," he said, turning toward the door.

I said nothing, an irrefutable fact.

DECEMBER 2016

I called my aunt on her birthday, which was also Christmas. I lived across the country, in a small town where they remember their dead with funerals in churches. I was walking my dog, unseasonably warm. I wished her happy birthday, and we talked about my job and my writing and my

stepchildren, and she sounded
the tiniest bit drunk, her
words just barely smudged on
the edges. I planned on asking her about it whenever we
next spoke, not on her birthday, but then I found myself
asking.

This was what I learned
about Hazel the last time I
spoke with my aunt, before
she died a few months later
of alcoholism: Hazel was
raped by her father. She sex-
ually abused my dead uncle,
her oldest, the one who was
bipolar in the generation before me.

Afterward, I called my
father. I wished him Merry
Christmas. I didn't mention
his mother. I didn't say anything about incest or abuse.
Instead, we talked about the
movies we'd watched, the
weather. No, it wasn't snow-
ing. It was sunny and clear, like
California. He talked to me

for exactly five minutes before saying he had to go.

Another thing about Hazel.
She gave horrible presents, a
set of silverware to a little boy.
One more reason my father
hates Christmas.

JULY 1928

It was summer, hot. I went
up to the attic, the hottest
but stillest room in the
house. Everything was so
loud, the kids playing, my
brothers bickering, Mama
clanking around the can-
ning jars. I just needed
some silence.

It was dusty, everything
brown, brown, brown, but
dark, too, the only light
coming from the small
round window in the
eaves. I started to read, but
quickly it felt like a change
in weather, the way the
leaves in the trees shake before a storm. That same old
sickness.

I lay on my stomach, not
caring about dirtying my
dress. I pressed my cheek
against the rough wooden
floor. And then I was rubbing my face against it,
wanting to scrape it, wear it

raw. I wanted the dust in my mouth, coating my tongue, the way it had been the very first time, in the ditch, with no way to name what was happening to me. I rubbed harder, higher, lower, my cheekbone, my chin, feeling the scrape, scrape, scrape of the wood. I opened my mouth, dragged my teeth. Still no grit. I stopped moving and just licked the floor with my tongue, a dog.

MAY 1935

I couldn't sleep, my body a mess of nerves. The house had been dead silent for hours. I got up, walked down the hall, down the stairs, out the kitchen door, quiet as a ghost. When I reached the mailbox I broke into a run, my bare feet crunching the grass, cool night air swimming through my fingers. At the top of the hill, I flung myself down, the air knocking out of my lungs.

The moon was a flat plate and my nightgown fluttered. The clouds in the sky were moving so fast you could see them changing shape, running from something. I felt myself being plucked like a guitar string, each moment a new emotion—here is boredom, here is joy, here is grief, here is shame—and I felt each note to my core, yet none of the feelings belonged to me.

MARCH 2018

After my aunt died, my cousin and I flew out to meet our great-aunt, Hazel's sister, for the first and likely last time. She was dying. It took an entire day to get there, an old house on an old road outside Helena, Montana.

My great-aunt had long crooked fingers and bright eyes, a creaky walker, and an oxygen tank. We slept upstairs in a single room with a set of twin beds, a floor she never went on anymore, and while the downstairs was neat and gleaming, the bedroom was covered in a thick scrim of dust. It was so dark that we left the night-light on while we slept, me in my narrow bed and my cousin in hers, like children.

We spent the days either on the porch, eating store-bought cakes and huddled under blankets, or in her basement, sorting through boxes of papers and photos and junk, preparing the house for her impending death. In between, my cousin and I tried to extract the facts of our family but got very little; the truth was impolite to verbalize.

The ancestors came from Germany and Ireland, circumstances of poverty and death. Possible gypsy blood. The German side: more incest. The lineage went back.

This was all interesting,

but I had come for Hazel. My great-aunt said she was a "problem child," a descriptor that could have also been applied to me and, for a briefer time, to my cousin.

"What did she do?" I asked, hoping for at least a gradient—did this mean bad grades or teenage pregnancy? Instead, she simply said that Hazel was "always getting into trouble," changed the subject.

Other extractions: My grandfather met Hazel in an upswing, the part of her arc where she was charming and effervescent. She got pregnant, they got married. After two decades of marriage, my grandfather asked my great-aunt, a trained therapist, for advice about getting her committed. They divorced instead.

On the last night, the temperature dipped below zero, and we plugged the cracks in the big window in our tiny bedroom with hand towels. We lay awake, despite our early flights, and I wanted to know my family better but mostly I was grateful to get home, to escape the feeling of decay and loneliness that cloaked everything in the house. I pretended the night-light was candlelight, I pretended we were in Nebraska, I pretended my cousin was my sister.

"What did your mom tell you about Hazel?" I asked her, a whisper, in case she had fallen asleep. But she sat up.

"She never really talked about her."

This surprised me. I had assumed that my aunt, the youngest, the only girl, was the only one who didn't hate her. The two of them alone in the house after the divorce, the boys already away at college.

"All I really got was that Mom felt like her mom's

caretaker, like she didn't get to be a teenager. I think that's why she was so obsessed with Facebook. Live out her teen fantasies or whatever, flirt with boys." She twisted her long dark hair behind her shoulder. "Apparently Hazel had seizures. Mom had to cradle her head in her lap and hold down her tongue so she wouldn't choke."

SEPTEMBER 1942

When we moved to California, I snuck out at night, after everyone was asleep. At first it was just to the beach, the strangeness of the ocean, glossy blackness and the white foam glowing blue under the moon. The way the water came in, went out, my ankles submerged, and then not. When I finally went back to my house, crawled into bed, I could still feel the rhythm of the waves on my body, lulling me like a baby in a rocker.

Later, I discovered the bar, a pull toward the

lights that were shining
farther down the beach.
Inside, mostly men, mostly
boys, all in uniform. Some
women, too, from the air-
plane factory, dirty hands
and coveralls. But I no-
ticed a few women like me,
women in skirts, so I sat at
the counter and ordered a
beer.

I didn't like beer. I didn't
like the way it tasted, like
my father, but I learned that
I liked the way it made me
feel. Made it easier to mold
my smile and my laugh into
the version that I wanted,
easy and free and bubbly.
Taught me just when to
put my hand on the men's
arms, the right amount of
pressure to trick them into
thinking it was unusual for
me to be in a bar, talking to
a strange man, our meet-
ing a freak occurrence, me,
such a nice girl. Sometimes

we'd go for a walk on the beach, my body warm and rustling from the alcohol. I let them hold my hand. I let them kiss me on the cheek. Sometimes, I let them do something more. I imagined them going back overseas, remembering me, not realizing I was actually a tramp and an old maid. I always looked younger and more innocent than I was, my one true gift.

An official date with a nice boy, home on leave. I liked him, might let him do more. But the beer did something strange that night, cast a spell on me, and in the boy's face I could only see my father, a man who would soon be dead. I excused myself, ran to the bathroom, vomited up the beer, but still the only thing I could taste was him. I took the soap from the sink, shoved it in my mouth, scrubbed around. Another woman came in the restroom, tall, glamorous, a mink stole. I spat in the sink. Bubbles. "Just brushing my teeth," I told her, forced a laugh. "Sometimes I can't stand the taste of beer."

She assessed me, knew I was lying, knew just by looking at me that I was full of it.

I snuck out the front door of that bar, never heard from the nice boy again. I walked home as quickly as I could without running, wanting to appear normal, but I caught my heel in a crack in the sidewalk and went spilling, my knee bleeding. The gravel in my mouth, the grit my teeth secretly longed for.

APRIL 2018

On my dead aunt's Facebook page, I found dozens of photo albums. She was a beautiful girl, a 1970s California babe with gleaming blond hair. Like at the memorial, there were old photos of her dead brother, her dead father, my father, my cousin, me, all of her ex-husbands. There were exactly two photos of Hazel. I printed them out.

NOVEMBER 1947

The day my oldest was conceived, Ted and I went out of town, just to get away. A beautiful day, something I still could not get over, even after living in California for five years: the sunshine, the temperature, the sky that shocking blue. I was driving, heading east to Anaheim, and I looked so good that day, my hair long in shining curls. Frankie Carle on the radio, my lipstick perfect. I kept looking across at Ted, his handsome face, laughing my practiced laugh at his jokes, and it came out just right every time. I was taking the turns a little too fast, but with control, and I could tell he was impressed by me—he, the star pilot. Everything perfect, perfect, perfect, like on the radio, like in the movies, and I thought my life was finally turning around, finally escaping that pit of a place, Nebraska. I kept looking at myself in the driver's mirror, and I looked like a movie star, a charming, glamorous girl, a dazzling spirit.

JUNE 2018

It was pouring rain the day I went to the library, my hair and hands wet as I sat down in the cheap plastic chair. I pulled up all the records I could find, her life a thin map of government bureaucracy. Census records, voting records, death records, divorce records. I googled the addresses I found, in Nebraska and in Los Angeles, but most no longer existed, except for one, a tiny bungalow by the beach. I tried to picture Hazel living in this house, so much different and bigger than the one in the town in Nebraska, but the only things I could imagine were pieces from movies, Raymond Chandler, and the Black Dahlia.

FEBRUARY 1959

Little Teddy could never sleep, even when he was a baby. A lot of times I wouldn't realize until I got up to use the bathroom, unable to sleep myself, and he'd call to me. I'd crawl in bed with him, turn on the globe light we kept by his bed, pull out a book and read to him, the heat of his little body next to mine. All I wanted to do was keep him safe, forever. Finally, he'd fall asleep, his blond hair gleaming so soft against his forehead.

It was just something that happened. He seemed so tense that day, so afraid and fearful, of nothing, and I wanted to soothe him. My hand in his pajamas, my body curling into him. I couldn't see his face but I heard his breathing, quickening before slowing down. He was too young to finish. Just a massage.

Afterward, he'd seize up like a deer whenever I walked in the room. I had sworn I'd never do it again. But the curse of me, the curse of my hand, always finding itself where it wasn't supposed to be.

JANUARY 1963

The fits increased in frequency. The doctors couldn't tell me where they came from, why they had begun so late in life. I was given medication; my driver's license was revoked. The pills made me fat, left a bitter film on my tongue. They blotted all the old rotten feelings out.

Of course I missed them. Everything else about me was dull, boring, normal. A housewife. A mother. A nice, well-kept home. I stopped the medicine. I had more fits.

One morning I awoke on the kitchen floor, my new slacks stained with piss. The children were at school. I'd chipped my tooth. I looked

AUGUST 2018

The only option left was to channel her. I recorded my efforts in a Word document. I wrote down the time, the date, and the methods. I tried meditation, tarot cards, burning things. I stared at her photos, holding her pin in my hand until it grew hot. In both pictures, she was smiling. In one, she wore a dotted dress, her hair a cloud of shiny curls around her head, a long pearl necklace. In the other, she was in her nurse's uniform, the pin I now held centered at her neck. In both, her eyes were sad, but in the first the sadness was overlaid with hope, while in the second there was only resignation. We didn't look much alike, except for the eyes, her cheeks round and soft while mine were all angles.

During this period I had in the mirror, told myself this gave my smile character. Changed into a skirt. Slicked on lipstick.

vivid dreams, strange because the medication I took usually blotted them out. I was in a field, in a place that might be Nebraska, and I looked down at my legs and they were filled with onions, long green onions that had somehow gouged my legs like needles, lightly trailing my calves with blood. I pulled them out, slowly, one by one, and it hurt. I dreamed I was a nurse, I had patients, the ordinary humiliations of losing one's life, diapers and colostomy bags, and I was panicking because I couldn't figure out which patient to attend to first.

The next morning, I stuck the nursing pin through the neck of my shirt. I stared at her photos on my dresser.

There was this hallucination I used to have, the bipolar disorder. I'd look in the mirror and not see my face, instead see a bird. It wasn't like my face was gone, there was simply an overlay of the bird, like a mask, feathered and quivering.

The room filled slowly with shadow, the hearing in one of my ears replaced by a hollow ringing. I looked at Hazel's smile, her soft-looking white skin, familiar features now. I placed my hand on the dresser, steadying myself, suddenly dizzy. I had wanted to understand the mysteries of her life, but I didn't really know what that meant. I looked in the mirror. I saw a cloud of curls, a long pearl necklace, a soft white curve of a cheek, overlaid on my face like a flickering mask. I understood the loneliness of the plains and the big city. I knew the loneliness of being overtaken by an unnamed force in your brain. I understood what it was to beat your kids, to rape them, to be raped by your father. I saw

AUGUST 1968

Later, years later, three kids raised, marriage doomed, I brought back that image of me on that perfect sunny day, in the car, with her smile, both hopeful and sad. I heard her voice. I heard her laugh. I recognized the sound of them.

Ted, still young, when I was feeling down. Trying to remember who I really was, not this sad, tired woman. I remembered the wind, the smell of the citrus, the way the sun gleamed but didn't sting. I remembered Ted's smile, the way he kissed me, the way I had charmed him without having to try.

But sometimes, the vision shifted. I saw the woman with the curls and the lipstick, but suddenly her hands were off the steering wheel, she turned to the camera, her face no longer wearing an easy grace but terror, a monster, the thing that had always been lurking inside of me. I saw her crashing the car into the orange groves, felt the jolt in my spine, the car turning over, the steering wheel puncturing my chest, the flames and smoke as our car exploded, both of us dead. And maybe that's what I should have done. Maybe our true destiny had been to die that day. The ghost of something that should have happened but didn't.

Other times, I saw a different person entirely, a stranger in the place of my face. Some young woman I didn't know. Black hair, heavy bangs, a little mouth. Angles in her cheeks where mine were round. She was always busy with something, deep in thought. It looked like she could have been writing something. I was never able to get her attention. I could not tell if she was aware of me, her face becoming mine, this strange woman, possessing me.

SAME PERSON, DIFFERENT FIRES

Witch Fire (2007)

She'd stopped taking her medication that summer. Now it was fall, her own small fire cranking up in her brain. She caught herself in the mirror, packing her toothbrush. Pupils wide, her face a pale sliver. She wasn't sleeping, wasn't eating, couldn't bring herself to slow down to do either. The fire was licking its way to the coast, the farthest west she could remember, a neighborhood usually protected by the wet cradle of the ocean. The emergency call had come thirty minutes before, a computerized voice instructing her to leave.

The first thing she'd done was smoke a cigarette, cross-legged on the floor, mind reeling, but not from the fire. Everything had happened so fast that autumn, the bridges she'd metaphorically burned, old friends and new friends and employers. The name of the fire felt like a joke, something she'd ignited with her thoughts. She couldn't remember if she, in fact, had willed it. Boyfriends had called her that before, a witch, her effect of giving the people sleeping next to her wild dreams. She'd felt it herself. Earlier that month, she'd been working her waitressing shift, cursing under her breath at the coworker she found so annoying. The next day, the coworker was dead. A semi had T-boned her car.

There was a part of her brain that recognized this was crazy thinking, the result of not taking the pills, her recurring delusion of a reverse messiah complex. Never did her brain tell her she was a savior. It only told her that she was a ruiner, possessing a divine talent for destruction.

She called a friend who was still talking to her, a short blond girl who was once her roommate, now living in one of the few neighborhoods that wasn't evacuated or burning or on alert. There was a fire near there too, but it was small and named blandly. This caused her to think it was safe, disconnected, a regular result of Santa Anas and downed power lines, as opposed to the Witch Fire, which felt plugged right into her. The friend offered the couch, what she'd been hoping for.

Bag packed, she got in the car, but instead of turning it on, she just sat there, eyeballs stinging from lack of sleep. Even her hands on the steering wheel looked skinny, bony and sharp like claws. She lit another cigarette, left it on the dash, got out, found a can to ash in. Normally she threw the butts out the window. This time, it wouldn't be her fault if there was another fire.

She turned the ignition, music blaring, her habit of listening so loud her ears hurt. It made her jump. It felt impossible to drive south to her friend's. Instead, she went up the hill, to the beach.

The parking lot, usually packed with tourists and buses of schoolchildren, was empty, a greasy McDonald's bag tumbling across the asphalt. The sky over the ocean glowed a dirty yellow, the sun not a sun but just a ball. At her back, there were the remnants of a city in flames.

Cedar Fire (2003)

She shut her thumb in the car door. It wouldn't have been as bad if the door wasn't locked, but it was, so she had to dig in her purse to get the keys. She resisted the urge to scream, unlocked the door, retrieved her hand.

The thumb looked fine at first, except for a stream of blood trickling out the bed of the nail.

She walked into the gas station, went to the counter with the hot dogs, and got a napkin to blot away the blood. It was already swelling red, the tip twice as big as it should be. The cashier looked at her warily from behind his sheet of plastic, taking in her crazed eyes and the fresh injury. She considered explaining to him what had happened but didn't.

Her boyfriend was taking her to see a band later that night. She tried to not make a big deal of her thumb when she got to his apartment, despite its angry pulsing while she drove, so swollen and sore that it was hard to steer. He noticed it right away, though. She brushed it off with a joke. But when she stood up from his sofa, she got so dizzy she had to sit right back down.

He insisted on the hospital, drove her to urgent care. The fires were far away, had just begun to turn the air, but the hospital was already chaotic with minor injuries, smoke inhalation, people with asthma and other breathing problems. The doctor only looked at her hand, decided it wasn't broken, told her to buy a splint at the drugstore. He wrote a prescription. She lied and claimed to be allergic to both ibuprofen and acetaminophen. He believed her, wrote a month's worth of OxyContin.

They laughed in the car, went to the Rite-Aid, took two each. It was dark now, the fire a blot on the horizon. He wrapped her thumb under the dim light of the parking lot.

At the bar, they bought drinks, waited on the patio for the opening band to finish. The Oxy kicked in at the same moment for both of them and they kissed, a giddy feeling light in their chests. The pills did their job. There was still pain in her thumb but now it was simply an object placed beside her. The winds changed, blew the ashes toward them, raining over the patio, powdery and white like snow.

Esperanza Fire (2006)

The hills were burning, so she left. In reality it was just an excuse, a reason to go. Redlands was hot stucco and hot cement, ratted grass and LA's dirty air. It was also rolling mountains and blooming trees, but in Redlands she was blind to beauty.

She threw a bag in her trunk, no work for three days and hopefully the city would be ashes when she was due back. Her car was shitty: no a/c, no power locks, not even power steering. No a/c in Riverside County was a mistake. She'd made worse.

An example: she didn't look at the news before she left. The freeway she took was the wrong one. The fires had spread too quickly to close the road. Four firefighters had died that morning. Another would die the next day. She didn't know this yet.

The hills were normally brown but now they were black, embers glowing like tiny stars. She was speeding as she passed them, streaks of red in her rearview. A different patch was still burning strong, close to the road, and she felt the heat of it ooze through the door. If another person believed in signs they might have seen it as a bad one, but she did not interpret it that way. Instead she took it as her being on the right path, away from her life, a tiny room that always felt on the verge of an implosion. Now it was dissolving behind her; soon enough, she would reach the coast.

The person who started the fire was later sentenced to death for five murders. He's still alive, though, at San Quentin.

Torrey Pines Fire (1992)

It was the first fall after they'd moved from the desert. Her new school had a view of the ocean. She hadn't made friends yet, too early in the year. The winds that nobody had told her the name of blew hot in her hair. Dry like the desert, familiar.

The adults called off afternoon classes, made scrambling phone calls to parents. Her mother and father were, of course, at their new jobs. She sat on a planter near the parking lot, watching the other children climb into minivans. Every time a silver car pulled in, she thought it was her mom, stood up to check. It wasn't. A small wave of panic slowly twisted in her chest, the possibility that her parents had burned, leaving her orphaned and forgotten.

The parking lot emptied. She was still sitting there, the only other person a boy she already knew not to talk to. He licked rocks, always wore the same sweatshirt regardless of the weather. The sky was brown. She pulled strips of bark off a tea tree, shredding them into papery threads with the dull tips of her fingers. The rocks in the planter were flecked with ash. She was resolving with herself that her parents would never come, that she needed to walk home, when her mother finally arrived in her silver car. A white rise of anger crawled up her throat, but she said nothing, just grabbed her backpack and sat in the car, staring blankly out the window.

Lilac Fire (2017)

California and its fires were behind her. Now she lived somewhere else, a place with floods and snowstorms and the occasional tornado. The type of disasters that couldn't be blamed on people or companies; these were deemed acts of God. Over the phone, her mother complained, they had to be ready to evacuate every year now. She watched the fires from a screen, trapped under glass in miniature like a snow globe. She felt a wisp of nostalgia, an empty longing for the proximity of tragedy, the dull sun, the burning air.

THE ARSONIST

When I moved to be with him, I didn't have a job. He left for hours and I was alone. The apartment was terrible, slapped together and flimsy. The carpet was industrial, worn thin, and the floor always felt so hard. He had no furniture, just a bed and a couch. But we got a bit of money from the wedding, so for the first few weeks I spent the hours at discount stores, buying lamps, an end table, a bookshelf.

Then the money was gone. Time rolled out in front of me, exhausting. I had no friends, no hobbies. Idle hands.

I got in my car. I popped in a CD, scratched with the title faded in Sharpie. I went for a drive around town, up the hill that made me carsick, down to the Walmart, out to the soccer field, and the feeling of idleness shriveled. The next day, a different route, a different CD. The day after that, I got lost. I pulled out my cell phone and typed in *Home*. I've always been so stupid when it comes to directions. I went out for a drive the next day anyway, and the next, getting lost and getting found, thanks to that lovely invention called a GPS. Every day I went driving, past the strip malls, the dingy houses, all the churches and their wide fat lawns. It ate up the time, gave me a sense of freedom.

That was the year the news first started reporting on the opioid epidemic. I saw it everywhere—foreclosed houses, unsupervised children, empty baggies tossed in parking lots, once, in the grass, a needle. One evening, not even dark yet, I was at the stoplight in front of Kroger, the single busiest road in town. A man stood at the corner. I watched him flick a lighter. Something glinted in the light, a square of tinfoil. A woman stood close to him, crooked her neck, breathed in a puff of smoke with a straw. I was shocked. All the years I'd spent in cities, renting apartments in bad neighborhoods. I'd never seen anything like that. Cops drove by this corner all the time.

The last day of summer, I accidentally slept till noon, woke up covered in sweat. I decided I'd go somewhere new, down to the river, this pretty spot we'd been to a couple times. When I left, it was the hour when the light is syrup, and with my music loud on the stereo I felt a small gust of air rise in my chest. The road out of town was two lanes, curvy, the type I didn't know how to drive on, used to freeways, but I was getting better. I still felt unnerved, though, whenever someone was behind me, worried my cautious speed betrayed my cityness. Everyone in this town had giant trucks. That day, a Chevrolet, headlights blazing, those stupid LEDs just high enough from the ground to blind you. I was going ten miles above the speed limit, but still the giant truck was right on my ass.

The line was double yellow when he passed me. I had my window down, all the unfamiliar smells of green, and he

was driving so fast the wind pressed against my face the
stench of burning tires and exhaust. I imagined a car coming out of nowhere, the Chevy driver dead, me dead, but
nothing happened. I read the sticker on his bumper before
he roared down the road. Big red font, WE DON'T CALL
911, an outline of a gun.

I got lost after that, made a wrong turn somewhere. The
narrow road narrowed further and the cliffs on the sides
seemed so high. I remembered the story my new husband
had told me, some aunt dying on a road like this, a fallen
boulder, right onto her car, crushing her, dead on impact. I
pulled out my phone, tried to type in *Home*, but, of course,
I had no service. I kept driving, hoping to find a straight
patch of road to turn on but there was nothing, just curves
and curves and switchbacks. The sun was starting to set,
the light fading to blue. I finally found a decent stretch of
road. I turned around. I had no idea where to go from there.
Finally, I saw a mailbox, a small dirt road leading up to a
house.

Their lawn was tidy, late-summer mums blooming. At
that point, my words hadn't yet loosened up and were still
rigid in their vowels. I knew it took only half a syllable for
me to be marked as an outsider, and I didn't want to end up
shot. But the woman—elderly, fat, floral—who opened the
door was sweet to me. I could smell something cooking in
her house, maybe onions, as she smiled and directed me to
town.

He was already home by the time I got there. I didn't want

to admit I'd gotten lost but otherwise my absence had no explanation. Fortunately he didn't seem to think anything of it, said nothing about me knocking on a stranger's door.

After that, I forbid myself from leaving the house unless I had to. But in the apartment, my life felt pointless and caged. It was a small complex, six units, next to what used to be a field but was now a construction site. They were building a new road, something called a Z-Way, and the view was brown dirt and orange cones. But there was still a bit of meadow and I walked down there.

There were a couple trees, skinny young maples, and this time of year, their leaves were skimpy and yellow. Tufts of grass, goldenrod plumes, but too much trash to mistake the tiny strip for nature. Empty beer bottles, McDonald's bags, a sock. Plastic pop bottles. I was learning to call it that, pop and not soda. There was something in one of the Mountain Dew bottles, and I thought about what I knew of shake-and-bake meth. The green plastic was cloudy.

I had been smoking in secret, only one or two when he went to work, and before he got home I took a shower. I hid the cigarettes in my underwear drawer, the way I had when I was a teenager. I lit a cigarette, took a drag. My mind was empty of thoughts when I picked up a piece of paper, one of those inserts with coupons, mottled and holed from old rain. I flicked the lighter. The flame kept going out, but finally it took. I added some dried scraps of brush and soon I had a fire. I sat down in the grass and watched it burn and then I stomped it out. The pile it left was black and ash.

I went back into the apartment, took a shower. Still wet in my towel, I peeled open two slats of the dusty miniblinds, expecting to see the field in flames, but there was nothing, same view as always: the parking lot, the dumpster, the skinny maples, the construction site that would become a road.

So that's what I did now when he left. I got to know the trash back there very well, crumpled paper, flyers and door hangers, empty cigarette packets, and a pamphlet from a church. I burned them all. I burned the sock. I left the cloudy Mountain Dew bottle alone. Soon the little field was pockmarked with black circles. Soon there was no trash left. I picked up a plastic shard of a shotgun shell, held the lighter, watched the plastic bead down.

One day I brought some trash from home, receipts, a cereal box that I tore into strips, a paid doctor bill. I pulled a ball of hair from my brush and I took everything into the field and then I lit it on fire. I ignited my hair last and it smelled so bad and I let it burn, snapping and popping. But then the wind came and took my hair away. It bounced into a bush, which was dead because now it was fall, and some of the leaves lit on fire. I always stomped the fires out with my boot but the patch in the bush was too high to stomp on. Breath short, I grabbed it with my fist, and the pain bloomed so hot and sharp in my palm and I felt it all the way in my toes, but it put the fire out. I waited until the wisps of smoke blew away, hand throbbing, and then I went back to the apartment and ran my hand under cold water. It blistered over.

It seemed funny that all my attempts to keep myself oc-
cupied always tilted over into miniature disasters. The fire
incident elicited one more self-ban. The next day when he
left I sat down to read, and then I made us an elaborate
dinner. I did this for the rest of the week: couscous, baked
chicken, chimichurri, homemade bread. But I felt the emp-
tiness creeping in and soon enough, I was back there, my
own trash in hand, ready to start another fire.

Right between two of my ash circles, I saw something
new, long and skinny, a stick. The blackness of a cleft hoof
and the short brown hair, skinned in a straight line like a
furry sock. The top of it was bare bone, neatly splintered. It
took me a second to register it as a single leg of a butchered
deer, still fresh. Ants crawled delicately over the thin skin. I
lit the fire. I plucked the leg up by the bone end, tossed it on
top, somebody else's kill, but mine to burn.

NATURAL SELECTION

The land she was born on was arid and dry. Sometimes she tried to keep a houseplant, something supposedly easy. It always died. Black thumb.

Eventually, she moved. The new place was green every time of year except for winter, which was white. The woods that surrounded her were so dense the plants bled into each other, flowers on top of ferns on top of trees. It was easy to be alive in the new place. All you had to do was go outside.

The first summer, a tomato plant. The next year, thyme and mint and peppers. Every year it grew bit by bit until she had a garden. She lived in an ordinary neighborhood, houses plopped on squares right next to one another, but her house was at the tail end and looked onto a sea of trees. The yard went from the tameness of the garden and gradually grew wilder: grass, oak trees, blackberry brambles, pokeberry and its fat red stalks. As the sun went down, she put on mosquito spray and tended her garden, clipping dead leaves, pinching buds, harvesting snips of herbs and fat vegetables, the twilight its dusky blue that tints everything with the pallor of the dead.

In pots, she sprouted exotic plants: night-blooming jasmine, holy basil, onions from seeds imported from Israel. She grew "vegetable neurotics," labeled as such in an old book from the library, lore going back to medieval times, belladonna and its jewel-black berries, henbane and its sunny flowers, plum veins etched in a warning. She handled the poison berries and flowers with gloves, and it felt like she had corralled it, caged a death force. The henbane waved its stinky purple-and-yellow face, complacent.

She took to sitting out there at night, enjoying the quiet lull of the plants. The frogs croaked in the creek, the cicadas trilled in the trees, sometimes a raccoon or maybe a fox screamed. The moon shone like a flashlight through the trees, searching. She was aware of some barely perceptible force hovering there, in the plants, in the woods, both weightless and heavy like a magnetic field, a wall building itself outside of her.

In the kitchen, she sliced the tomatoes and cucumbers, made salads of lettuce and kale. It felt good to eat things she had created from her own hand, things she had transformed into life. Or so she thought.

One night she was under the weather, tired, some sort of weird summer cold. She sat in the garden in the dusk and fell asleep. The moon rose in the sky, cutting through the trees until it was straight over her. The jasmine opened its petals, sweet scent sticky in the air. In her dreams, the plant tendrils reached over her, the briars from the berries tangling her hair. While it was true that the garden wouldn't be there without her, what that really meant was right *there*, pruned in pots on her patio. The plants had grown from soil, not her hand. They existed coldly, with indifference, separate from her.

From then on, they invaded her dreams, appeared in front of her eyelids as soon as they shut: branches unfurling, leaves spreading, until they constricted her like a strait-jacket, choking her with ball gags of flowers. The blackberry brambles pushed thorns into her skin, drawing blood. The pokeberry stalks snapped and stained in streaks. Every night, the same dreams. She still tended to her garden, now only in the safe light of day, out of a sense of obligation rather than joy. This was the bed she had made. When she ate the vegetables, it now gave her the feeling of a hunter skinning prey, violent and primordial.

Soon summer was over. She considered taking some plants indoors as she had done in the past but decided it wasn't worth the dirty countertops. The plants could go the way of nature. A time for everything, including death.

The cucumbers and holy basil went first, fragile leaves withering in the cold. Then went the tomatoes and peppers. Eventually, the garden was just sticks, dead leaves plucked off by the wind, rotting in the soil. She stood from her kitchen, where she had a view of the patio, the plants all helpless and dusted with snow. A feeling of triumph rose in her chest. She had conquered them, a jealous god.

What she didn't consider was that their death had not come from her. This was all tied together in something more powerful, a greater orchestration beyond her control. It was she that was tamed, dependent on electric heat, running water, a warm bed, not the plants. And someday it would be her turn to rot in the soil.

LITTLE BITCH

The first time the woman met Ruby was before the wedding. She was the older child, just turned four. Ben was still a baby, so he stayed home. It was winter. Ruby was bundled in a hat and jacket, a pink puffy ball, wide brown eyes and messy curls.

The woman had brought a present, some fancy paint markers. The label said they were appropriate for Ruby's age, but she just looked at them warily. The father, the woman's new fiancé, turned on *Daniel Tiger*. He went to the fridge, handed Ruby a bowl of strawberries, a cup of juice. The woman tried to engage with the child. Instead, Ruby watched TV. She ate strawberries. She drank juice.

The woman took the markers out of the box. She had no experience with children, didn't yet know the danger of expectations, their nature of being wild and unpredictable. Because she didn't know better, she put the markers on the table, beside a stack of paper, thinking this would lure Ruby in.

Ruby looked at the markers. She picked one up. The woman felt happy, imagined drawing pictures together, bonding, becoming friends. But Ruby merely stood the single marker up on its fat base, like a doll. It toppled over. She went back to the TV.

A second later, the child began making a retching sound, like a cat with a hair ball. The woman watched pink paste dribble out of Ruby's mouth. Strawberries and apple juice. She was still too young to know how to throw up properly, that you're supposed to lean your head over. The vomit dripped down her neck. The woman didn't know what to do with the sudden mess. The father raced over, picked up Ruby, opened the front door, deposited her on the porch. Ruby was now crying and screaming, the cruelty of being a human in the world.

The woman followed them, wanting to help. She stood there, watching, more pink vomit bubbling out of the child's mouth. The father wasn't looking at the woman. He was trying to keep Ruby's hair out of the puke. The woman went back inside, wet some paper towels. Ruby was done with the puking now but not the crying. Her dad carried her upstairs, not noticing the paper towels, put the child in the bathtub, cleaned her off, replaced her clothes. The woman sat in the living room by herself, still holding the wet paper towels, staring blankly at the TV, useless.

They were married a few months later. She moved across the country to be with him, leaving the city for a small town. Her new apartment was spartan, the place her husband had moved when he got divorced from his first wife, lonely and defeated. His mother had given him some things, pots and pans, and his ex-wife let him keep some things, a sofa, the TV. He had only bought the things that were absolutely necessary, a dish sponge and a shower curtain. Beyond that, the place was empty. The woman busied herself unboxing the gifts that had arrived for their wedding. Soon the apartment had bookshelves, a blender, pictures on the wall. Soon it became more of a home.

On the weekends, they went over to his parents' house with the kids, an hour away in an even-smaller town. The grandmother usually cooked the meals, roast beef and fried chicken and mashed potatoes, and, at night, she usually gave the kids their baths. The woman felt guilty, like she wasn't being a responsible adult, some kind of leech on their resources. The husband explained. This was a different culture, the importance of extended family. He said that a lot: California, where she'd come from, was a different world than here in West Virginia. The woman was experiencing culture shock, he told her. She didn't believe him. They were in the same country in the same year, with the same Starbucks and Subways dotting the freeways. Except here they were called "interstates."

But her new in-laws didn't seem to mind. They tried to make the woman feel like a part of the family, asked her questions and explained the context of the things they said. The woman still felt lost. She could barely understand her new father-in-law's accent. She didn't know the cultural references, had never heard of the Statler Brothers or the old movies they watched on TV. She didn't know the people they discussed or their relationship to her husband. All she knew was everybody they talked about was either dying or dead.

The stepson, Ben, was easy to win over. Quickly he became his new stepmother's buddy, curling into her lap, grabbing her books and pretending to read them, toddling along with her on walks, until he grew tired and then she carried him. He elicited something in her she didn't know she had, an ability to nurture children.

Ruby, on the other hand, was a whole other matter. She didn't look at the stepmother when she spoke to her. Instead, she stared off into the distance, warily, like she was gazing at some holy power. If the stepmother pressed it, tried to engage her in conversation, Ruby just screamed, "No no no no no no no. Leave me alone!" The woman tried not to take it personally. Ruby yelled a lot, not just at her. But it still hurt.

On Saturdays, they all went to McDonald's, one of only three options for restaurants in the tiny town. The family worked as a team: the father ordering the food, the grandmother wiping the grimy tables, the grandfather getting the ketchup and napkins. There was nothing for the woman to do. So she stared at the other customers, old men with oxygen tanks, young men in fatigues or muddy boots, another family of six praying before their meal, a Glock strapped to the father's waist, barely visible under his gut. The woman never ate McDonald's before she'd come here, but still she knew that the customers in California didn't look like this. Maybe her husband was right after all. Maybe this was an entirely different country. She was an interloper, a random piece plopped next to a random family.

A few weeks later, the woman and her new husband went to see Ben play baby soccer. They all sat together, mismatched: Ben and Ruby, the ex-wife and her new husband, a surgeon, and the babysitter, a cute graduate student at the local extension of the state university. The ex-wife wore an expensive sweater, carried a designer purse. The woman felt uncomfortable, having just come from her new job. She sat in a folding chair, tugging at her cheap pencil skirt to hide the lining. The ex-wife made jokes, wanting to make the woman feel welcomed. She leaned back in the chair, tried to relax. The soccer game was ridiculous, the kids too young to grasp the concept, barely old enough to run.

Ruby was curled up in the babysitter's lap, playing with her iPad. She saw the woman looking at her, stared vaguely in her direction. She softly touched the babysitter's face, stroking her cheek. The woman felt jealous, couldn't imagine being the recipient of Ruby's affection.

Ruby got out of the babysitter's lap. She put her iPad on an empty chair, standing over it. She began to do the thing she always did, with books and the iPad, pressing her face close to their flat surface, as though she could punch herself into their world, away from the mommies and stepmommies

YOU ARE THE SNAKE

and babysitters, replaced by balloonish cartoon characters and songs. This was always accompanied by a noise, a long sustained *uhhhhhhhheheheeeehhhhh*. She jumped up and down, waving her hands, flapping.

The woman knew what that flap meant. Her mom had taught kindergarten for twenty-five years, her best friend back in California taught special ed. Autistic kids. They flapped. She wanted to mention this to the mother but decided it was none of her business. Ruby wasn't yet diagnosed. The mother had made an appointment, though, three months in the future, to take Ruby to a specialist, hours away at the university, because in this town everyone traveled if they needed anything more than a routine medical procedure.

The "game" concluded, not after four quarters but when the children seemed tired. The family walked back to their cars. The woman and her husband helped the mother and stepfather load the folding chairs into the trunk of their luxury SUV. They waved goodbye to the children, who were already strapped in their car seats by the babysitter. They got in their own car, a practical, bottom-of-the-line sedan. They smiled at each other.

"That went okay, right?" the husband asked.

"That was fun," the new wife said.

It had been fun, she told herself.

The next weekend, Ruby was reading a book in the sitting room, with fancy couches and frilly decorations and a clock that her grandfather had built himself. The woman hadn't known anyone with a sitting room before. This one went against the stereotypes the woman had picked up about sitting rooms from movies. There were no plastic slipcovers over the couches. Ruby was free to play in there by herself, messing up the crocheted blanket and lacy pillows.

The woman had been in the back bedroom all day, reading. Sitting on the bed was making her back hurt. She went into the living room, but the men were watching sports, the loud voices of the announcers. She held her book, feeling helpless. There were no other rooms to read in.

She decided to risk it, went and sat in the sitting room, as far away from Ruby as possible. She didn't look at the little girl. She didn't want to upset her.

Ruby was doing her usual thing, standing over her favorite book, a fat collection of nursery rhymes, pressing her face close to the pages, making the noise, *uhhhhhhhhheheheeeehhhhh*, jumping up and down, flapping her hands.

Suddenly, she stopped jumping. She stared at the woman. The woman pretended not to notice, sitting quiet and still, intently gazing at her own book. It felt like dealing with a feral cat, no eye contact because she didn't want to startle the skittish thing. Ruby returned to the nursery rhymes, accepting her presence. The woman had won this round, a small victory.

Later, the woman and the husband went to the gas station to purchase energy drinks. The woman added a candy bar at the last minute. She ate junk food only on the weekends. The cashier handed the husband the change, smiled, told them both, "Be careful out there."

The woman and the husband walked back to their car, popping their energy drinks.

The woman felt a small blip of panic, imagining a storm on the way, a criminal on the loose. "Why'd the cashier say that?" the woman asked.

"What?" the husband said.

"Why'd she tell us to be careful?"

"Oh," the husband said. "I dunno."

They got into the car, the woman turning the phrase over in her mind, trying to discern the meaning.

Back in their bigger small town, the woman kept her ears open. Her bank was the old-fashioned kind, previously unfamiliar to the woman, where you place a paper slip into a tube, press a button that sends the tube to the teller, and then the teller sends it back with cash. "Be careful," the teller's voice said from the ratty speakers. The cashier at the grocery store said it, handing over a receipt. The receptionist at the school where she worked. *Be careful, be careful, be careful.*

One day the woman was standing at the front of the classroom, opening her book in preparation for a lecture on William Blake. One of the students approached her, a quiet girl from a nice family who got all As. "Caleb can't come to class today," she said. "A tree fell into his truck on the way to school." She pulled out her cell phone, showing the woman a photo taken presumably by Caleb, a big oak tree smashed into the windshield of a pickup truck. The girl told her he was fine, but his car was undrivable.

The phrase *Be careful* popped in her head. It clicked.

"I understand now," the woman told her husband when she got home. "You guys are just saying goodbye."

"What?" the husband said.

"Why everyone tells you to be careful," the woman said. "In California they tell you to have a nice day." Sterile, *nice* California. "But here, they tell you, 'Be careful.' A friendly reminder that you could die at any time." She told the husband the story about the student who hadn't made it to class.

"The life of a hillbilly is an intense life," the husband said. He was always saying that. The woman realized for the first time that this was true. He hadn't been lying. This was a different culture.

The woman decided she would get Ruby to like her the next weekend. She knew from her mother, the retired kindergarten teacher, and her best friend, the special ed teacher, that autistic children like playing with mushy things. The woman went to Walmart, bought some Play-Doh. It was a special set, flecked with glitter.

It was nice on Saturday, sunny and mild. The woman took Ruby out on the patio to play with the Play-Doh. She helped Ruby with the packaging. She felt surprised opening the lids, the perfect cylinders of dough, the synthetic smell, something she didn't know she remembered from childhood. She pinched off a chunk, handed it to her stepdaughter. Ruby took it, making her weird noise, *ehhhhhhhh*.

They sat at the table together, the woman mushing up another piece of Play-Doh. She shaped it into a neat heart, handed it to Ruby. Ruby accepted the heart, looking her directly in the eye, as though she were finally seeing her. The woman's stomach fluttered, reminding her of high school, the thrill of having the mean popular girl say something nice. It was happening. They were bonding.

Ruby placed the Play-Doh heart gently on the table, tried to make a heart of her own. The woman thought about helping her, decided against it. Instead, she busied herself making a chocolate chip cookie, a flat circle with little lumps of "chocolate chips." She started humming to herself, feeling peaceful and happy in the sunshine, playing with her new friend.

Ruby suddenly stopped messing with the Play-Doh. She stood up. She stepped closer to the woman, whose heart felt like it might burst out of her chest from happiness, imagining Ruby touching her softly on her face, the way she had done with the babysitter.

But Ruby didn't do this. Instead, she smacked the woman across the mouth. "No singing," she said.

The smack wasn't hard enough to hurt, but she still recoiled in surprise, dropping the incomplete Play-Doh cookie.

The husband had apparently been watching from inside. He opened the door, rushed onto the porch. The woman felt embarrassed, as though she deserved the smack. The husband grabbed Ruby by the hand, led her inside, chewed her out. The woman tried not to care. She picked up the cookie. It was dotted with dirt. The woman tried to remove the dirt but it wouldn't come off. She shoved the Play-Doh back in its container, the neat cylinder ruined, the sting of the slap still fresh on her mouth.

After dinner, the three of them went to the GoMart. The woman and Ruby waited in the car. The husband went inside to buy two energy drinks, and Skittles for Ruby. The woman looked down at her nails. They looked good, long and freshly painted, a pale purple with sparkles that reminded her of the My Little Ponies she'd had as a girl. She thought about earlier, the smack, her unforgivable offense of daring to make a noise. She suddenly felt angry, uncomfortable, this mean little girl having so much control over her emotions. She turned around, looked right at Ruby. The little girl had been singing a nursery rhyme. Nobody else was allowed to sing, but Ruby could sing constantly, the same thing over and over, annoying. Ruby stopped singing. She looked a little scared.

"You like my nails?" the woman said. Her voice came out nasty, taunting.

Ruby said nothing.

"Oh," the woman said. "I get it. You're jealous." She laughed, waved her fingers.

Something in Ruby's eyes changed, a flicker.

The woman turned back around, tucked her hands neatly in her lap. "Little bitch," she said. She had meant to just quietly mumble it, but she said it too loud.

She turned around again, hoping Ruby hadn't noticed that her new stepmother called her a bitch.

But Ruby heard her. She held the woman's gaze. She smiled. She laughed. She loved it.

The next time they had the kids, they stayed at the apartment. The woman's in-laws had gone out of town, a visit to a sister in Tennessee. The woman had bought kid food the night before, macaroni and cheese, sugary cereal, apple juice, strawberries for Ruby.

They decided to all go to Walmart, get the kids some toys. Ruby got in the cart even though she was too big, thighs pressing against the baby-sized slats. Ben wanted to walk, holding his father's hand to steady himself. The woman pushed Ruby in the cart, into the store, past the clothing, to the toy aisle.

Ben selected his toy first, a lightsaber that made different noises. The adults both realized this was a mistake but said yes anyway, the woman figuring she could hide the toy if it became too annoying. She had learned by then that kids are dumb, have short memories.

They went to the girl-toys aisle next. Suddenly the cart's

wheel jammed up. The woman reflexively kicked the wheel. The cart jostled, Ruby's little body moving backward and then forward.

The man turned around, looked at the woman, confused. "What happened?" he said.

"The wheel. It got stuck," she said. "But I kicked it. I kicked it into shape."

She did not say this, though, in her sterile Californian accent. Instead, she said it like a West Virginian, unnecessary vowels thrown in, mutilating the words until they were barely discernable: "Aye keecked it. Aye keecked it into shaeype."

The woman clapped her hand over her mouth, shocked at what had creeped out, somebody's voice that was not her own.

The man and the woman both started laughing.

Ben looked up at them, laughing too, even though he didn't understand the joke.

The woman's eyes weren't on Ruby, who was sitting quietly in the cart. She didn't see Ruby extend her arm, or the woman might have jumped, anticipating another smack.

But Ruby didn't hit her. Instead, she smiled, touched her stepmother's cheek. She gently stroked her face.

SANTA MUERTE

For Roberta Elam

Sister Teresa had not always been a good girl. She was rotten when her siblings were born, the oldest of seven, enacting small cruelties like hiding their toys, jumping around corners to scare them and make them cry. At school, she found minor trouble: talking back in class, drawing disturbing pictures of things like witches in art. There was the time she brought a new pack of pencils to class, glossy yellow with perfect pink erasers and neat, factory-sharpened tips. Rarely did she receive new things. In between periods, she left one on her desk. When she came back, it was gone. She found it in a classmate's hand, a beautiful girl who always had new everything. Teresa felt the familiar burp of anger expand in her chest until it reached her throat. The action she made in response was calculated, waiting for the girl to look out the window before grabbing it from her hand. Then the pencil became a weapon, that factory-sharp tip, dulled only by a few hours of writing, poking the girl on her lean white thigh. The girl shrieked and Teresa was given three days' detention, even though the pencil had been stolen from her, even though the lead hadn't pierced the skin.

She didn't behave in church, either, refusing to bow her head or cross herself. In the Bible, she scratched out words, replacing them with others—*poop, snot, stupid*—but for this she was mysteriously never caught. She liked the holy water, though, the familiar act and the cool wetness on her forehead.

And then there was the incident with the bird. She was in the canyon behind her house, had run away from her mother's request to tend to her siblings. She needed a minute alone. There, in the middle of one of the familiar paths, lay a baby sparrow, fallen, helpless, just beginning to get its feathers. Teresa crouched down, inspected the bird, its dumb blind eyes, its orb of a head, the weak chirping that came from its throat. It wasn't an act she thought about beforehand. She simply placed her palm over the bird, as though she might cradle it, but instead she pressed against its tiny body, hard. The baby bird's fine bones cracked. She pulled her hand away, first horrified, then fascinated. The bird was still alive but just barely. She found a rock and finished it off before tucking the bloodied body in a thick clump of bushes, washed the mess off her hands as soon as she got home. The image of the bird often came back to her, unbidden, at quiet times: on walks to school, in bed at night, while she was supposed to be bowing her head in church. Each time, she tried to bop the thought away, bury it down where it couldn't bother her, but a few days or weeks or months later, there it was again, bubbling back up. Crack of bones, splat of blood, the blurring line between life and death.

For many girls, the real troubles begin in puberty, but with Teresa there came a settling. The summer she turned twelve, she found herself finally accepting her role as the eldest, helping with the meals and the minding and the brushing of hair, without her mother even needing to ask. She began to pay attention in school, suddenly filled with a voracious curiosity, answering questions in English and history and even in Bible study. She was filled with a desire to help, gave her sandwich to a classmate who had forgotten his lunch, voluntarily loaned out her pencils. The change was gradual and then sudden. By the time Teresa was fifteen, she was so sweet to her siblings that the three youngest couldn't remember her being a terror at all.

It was in church, though, where the shift became most evident. The Bible, previously so boring and illogical, soon became a book of contrasting light and shadow. She read passages, culling sentences and turning them over in her mind, teasing out the meaning. And that was what she now liked most about the Bible, the fact that it was personal, a living, breathing thing that never ceased to catch her in the throat with surprise. She began to stay after Mass, met the priest in his office, where they debated passages and he told her about their history. It was there, in that tiny room next to the big church, that he asked her to help with meals they served the poor, and it was there that Teresa learned the pleasure of giving, the warmth in her heart that came from feeding the multitude.

By the time she was sixteen, Teresa no longer accepted presents on her birthday or Christmas, requesting that money be donated to the church's soup kitchen instead. After school, while watching over her siblings, she read the papers, informing herself about the horrible acts of man—wars, murder, greed. At night, she prayed over these atrocities, big and small, with the quiet knowing that God could ease the sufferers' pain, bring peace. Sometimes at night she even prayed for the bird, tried to replace the image of it, smashed and dead, with a healthy bird, praying for its soul to reach heaven, even though the Church taught that humans were uniquely cursed and blessed in having souls.

Soon Teresa arrived at the time where she had to decide what she wanted to do with her life. She knew she didn't want to get married, at least not yet, possibly ever. Strange men repelled her. She toyed with the idea of college, teaching, social work, maybe nursing school. But in none of these possible futures could Teresa actually see herself. Which is where this story actually begins: Teresa's decision to join the Church.

♦

Because Teresa had already done so much work with the Church, through her study sessions, her regular attendance at Mass, and her acts of charity, the priest was comfortable recommending her for pre-novitiate candidacy, despite her missing some of the basic requirements. He submitted a formal request to the archbishop so Teresa could be granted an exception.

Teresa prayed very hard, and her prayers were granted with favor. The exception was made. Teresa was sent north to the Sisters of Notre Dame de Namur Carmelite in Carmel-by-the-Sea.

It was in Carmel that Teresa learned she loved to run. Sister Rosalie took to Teresa immediately, and she to her. Sister Rosalie was keen on the idea of exercise as duty, the need to be thankful for the blessed body that God had given them. And so Teresa rose with the sun. Her body still laden with sleep, she laced her running shoes, exited the convent when it was still dark. The convent was right on the coast. That early in the morning, the ocean was still purple, the crash of the waves still violently loud, a wall of white noise that blotted out anything else. Teresa's lungs filled with the same briny air she'd known since childhood, and although she was now several hours from her mother and father and all her siblings, the smells and sounds of the ocean brought Teresa peace, the gentle cradling of her home, California.

One morning, only a couple weeks into her stay, she went on her usual run. She always ended by going as fast as she could for the final turn on the main road, until she reached the cypress tree in front of the convent. By then, she was covered in sweat, red-faced, shaky, her heart feeling like it might lurch out of her chest. She stood there, bent over and panting, until her breath and heart slowed down. She stretched for a while before walking back to the convent, body electrified, mind purified. But that day, it struck her that something was wrong. The sun had risen and now the ocean was blue and the sky was blue and the sand was tan and the trees were dry from drought, bent and rusted. It was the same world as her whole damn life, the same ocean, the same salty smell, the soil beneath her feet not soil but sandstone. She'd never felt like she'd truly fit in, here in her home state. It was too fair and too easy for her soul, which, despite its new infusion from God, felt like one inexplicably born from tumult, thunderstorms.

She had to hurry back to the convent to shower and eat before morning mass, but that day she did not feel like hurrying. Instead, she knew she needed to pray. And so she did, sitting on the rock wall that made up the entrance to the convent, head bowed, running the beads of her rosary through her fingers.

God granted her the vision almost immediately. He showed her a flash of images, like a slide reel: green grass, brick buildings, rolling hills, morning fog creeping through low mountains, trees that stood high and straight, unlike the gnarled trees she was used to. She quickly identified the images as her true spiritual home, a clear and certain stamp of destiny.

Mother Superior was surprised to see Teresa at the door of her office, still sweaty in her running clothes. She was even more surprised to hear what Teresa had to say, her certainty that this was not where she belonged. But Mother also knew the exact place that Teresa was describing from her vision. Normally a change so dramatic would be something she would instruct a person to pray over, but Teresa's vision was so clear and specific that it could only be a gift from God.

Two days later, Teresa got on a jet with a single suitcase, bound for Wheeling, West Virginia. It was her first time on an airplane, and the lurch in her stomach as the plane rose from the ground made her feel giddy. She was served a cola by a woman in a short dress. When she exited the plane on the tiny stairs, she tried not to feel like Jackie Kennedy, resisted the urge to raise her palm and wave weakly like a celebrity. She was glad she didn't. The new Mother Superior was waiting for her, would have seen her petty display of vanity.

Teresa was surprised by how the sisters treated her at first. They looked at her coldly; they'd heard things about Californians and their sinful acts, sex and drugs. They ribbed her accent, which especially surprised Teresa because she hadn't known she even had one, but it was true that she spoke differently than the women around her, with their snipped consonants and mangled vowels.

It probably didn't help that her hair was blond and pretty, that her face had a golden glow from her runs. The second day she was there, she borrowed a pair of scissors and cut off her hair just below her ears. As she lay in bed that night, she prayed, unsure that she was indeed in the right place. But God assured her. This discomfort was part of His plan.

The next morning, Teresa woke early, went on an explor-
atory run around the compound. It was summer, and Teresa
was completely taken aback by the feeling of the air, wet and
heavy like a breathing thing. But there was fog rolling off
the mountains like in her vision, and as Teresa began to
sweat she became aware of her place in things, just another
wet breathing being. She had never felt so far away from the
person she thought herself to be, the brown hills and her
large family. She had never felt so close to God. Tears ran
down her cheeks, and it felt like she was vibrating, her whole
body alive in the sacred act of prayer, the first time she understood the true meaning of praying without ceasing.

The sisters warmed up to her quickly enough. They
stopped commenting on the way she pronounced words.
They quietly noticed that she didn't actually think she was
better than them, eagerly washing dishes, peeling potatoes,
cleaning floors. When she weeded the garden, she didn't shy
away from getting her hands dirty. She brushed back her
hair when it strayed loose from her habit, leaving a smear of
dirt on her perfect tanned face, which stayed for the rest of
the day, because she was not so vain as to look in mirrors.

Soon she made a friend, Mary Grace, another woman
who had followed a path similar to hers, minus the part
about California. She, too, had gotten in trouble as a child,
denied her faith, but her denial was because she was from
the southern part of the state, some nowhere town called
Beckley. Mary Grace said there were hardly any Catholics
there. In school, the other girls pulled her hair, pushed her

down, told her she would burn in hell, ideas about false idols, the medallion of the Virgin Mary that she wore around her neck. But in high school, she got a scholarship to a tiny Catholic school. There, she was no longer a freak, and it was there that she truly learned to love Jesus. Like Teresa, it was in her senior year in high school that she felt the calling.

Mary Grace began to run with Teresa in the mornings, having participated in track in high school. She knew all the best paths already. Because it was summer, anything untamed was a wall of green—lime, emerald, kelly—so many shades Teresa was unaccustomed to, the coolness leaching from so many trees. She saw animals that had previously only existed for her in storybooks: deer, turtles, chipmunks. Birds, too, robins pulling worms, hummingbirds with scarlet chests, blue jays and their sharp beaks, once an oriole, alarming with its neon shade of orange. A part of her wanted to stop and observe these new things, these unusual shocks of beauty, but mostly she just wanted to keep going. The few times she did, Mary Grace laughed at her, amazed at her amazement at this ordinariness. Teresa soon began walking up the hill to pray after her run, alone, gazing at the trees and the mountains and all the living things in the woods. Sometimes she felt like something was looking back at her, from the trees, but she took it to be the presence of God, alive in every last little molecule that made up this earth, the ever-present caress of the Lord. In the morning sun, when she closed her eyes, she could see the tender face of Jesus.

Mary Grace and Teresa spent so much time together that their periods began to sync up, both beginning at the full moon, which Teresa took as a sign; they were close to each other, close to nature, close to God. It was another message telling her she was in the exact right place. But while Teresa's periods were light, painless, Mary Grace's laid her up in bed for a day, sometimes two. Teresa woke one morning to blood in her underwear and knew that Mary Grace wouldn't join her running that day. She brushed her teeth, put on her running clothes, went to the nurse's station, grabbed two aspirin, and went back to the dorm. She put the pills on the bedside table next to Mary Grace with a glass of water, kissed her gently on the forehead. She was suddenly struck with an odd feeling, like she was saying goodbye. She shook it off. It was probably just a blue mood, her period. Mary Grace stirred from sleep, groaned in pain. She smiled, accepted the aspirin. "I'll skip today," she said.

It was an especially beautiful morning. Teresa could tell the day would be a hot one, but right now the light was soft and golden. A family of deer cut through her trail, then stared back at Teresa as she passed, unafraid. There were butterflies and bees drinking drowsily from the flowers in the meadow. Teresa thanked God for the beauty, said a prayer as she ran.

After her run, Teresa was hungry so she grabbed an apple from the kitchen, then headed up the hill to continue her communion with God. It was starting to get hot, the sun rising blankly in the sky. Teresa normally sat in the grass, but today she decided to sit on the bench in the shade. She opened her prayer book, read for a few minutes, closed her eyes.

◆

Teresa didn't have a chance. The Bad Man knew she came there every morning after her run, alone. He knew the routines of the convent, that the rest of them were all inside at this time, that nobody would notice Teresa's absence until it was too late. The Bad Man knew the exact moment to walk out of the trees. He was only fulfilling a small part of his destiny.

Teresa didn't see him, or hear him, eyes still closed, thoughts on God. When she first felt his hands on her wrists, she mistook them for the touch of His hands on hers, letting her know He was there, He was listening, she was in the exact right place, this convent in far-off West Virginia. And He was indeed there, although it was impossible to know how this fit into His plan. Teresa knew that God was both loving and wrathful, and that it was futile to guess whether something horrible happened because He intended it to or simply because He was looking away. She screamed and fought, also a part of her destiny but not of the Bad Man's plan. The Bad Man tenderly wrapped the rope—he had only intended to bind her wrists—around her throat instead. After that, everything became easy. Teresa felt the pressure on her neck, recognized that she was no longer able to breathe. He needed her life now.

IS IT JACKAL OR IS IT DRAGON

There is empty space in each atom of the body. Dust is skin cells, pollen, smoke, and dirt drifting through the air to accumulate on flat surfaces. Wi-Fi produces an invisible film. A television composes an image through thousands of dots. Lights turn on because electrons move slowly up wires, about an inch per minute, while protons and neutrons are sedentary. Tap water carries arsenic, lead, antidepressants. Cement expands under the heat of the sun. Roots push through dirt in straight lines. Ants rub antennae to smell the air. Firefly larvae eat snails after injecting a fluid that numbs them. Plants alter their metabolism in response to threats. A woodpecker's tongue wraps around its brain, providing a protective cushion. Vultures prevent the spread of disease due to the acidity of their stomachs. Trees communicate through pheromones. Mountains grow thinner, pushed apart by water and wind. Clouds carry millions of gallons of water over hundreds of miles. The thermosphere can reach two thousand degrees Celsius, but the density is too low to conduct heat. The gravitational pull of the moon keeps the earth stable on its axis. Magnetic fields entangle the sun, producing solar flares, which disrupt power grids and pipelines. Supernovae increase biodiversity.

Energy cannot be created or destroyed, only transferred. This is a basic fact. The true color of the sky is violet, but the limitations of my eyes cannot see it. I breathe out, expelling the gas in my lungs. I light an object on fire. I see a person sneeze, and my immune system increases its response. I try to peel an apple but instead I peel my skin. I tear the ligaments in my knee. I receive corrective surgery in my mouth and my left hand. I become emotionally unstable because there is an excess of chemical receptors in my brain. I draw lines on dry pulp, and then I recycle it. I fly across the sky in a jet. I tap a button and pixels appear in a white box. I trap a spider to set it free. I tell elaborate lies to people I've never met. I grow flowers so butterflies can drink their nectar. I pay a stranger to insert wires and plastic into my uterus. I ask the internet to tell me how many times a jackal appears in the Bible, and it complies. Twenty, usually with owls, although sometimes the word תַּן is translated as *dragon*. Each action of mine is one small breath toward a flame. A hundred people die every hour.

I take money out of an ATM, put it in my wallet. It is 69 degrees and sunny. My mother is two thousand three hundred and eighty-three miles away. I am twenty million minutes old, a number that is mostly true for two years. Twilight is a liminal state, but so is everything. In the scheme of things, I will be dead soon, and no one will miss me. In the scheme of things, I never existed.

ACKNOWLEDGMENTS

First and foremost, I want to thank Scott McClanahan, my first and best reader, the greatest writer I know, a literal genius, and the person who has given me a life filled with happiness and purpose.

Thank you to the team at Soft Skull, for being such a beacon for so many decades. It is an honor and a dream to be published by and work with you all.

Thank you to Monika Woods, for your years of championing, advice, and tenacity.

Thank you to my family: my parents, Meg and Jerry; my stepmother, Nina; and my West Virginia family, Karen, Gary, Iris, and Sam. Your love and acceptance have given me so much strength, stability, and comfort.

Thank you to Sunny Katz, Alana Trinkle, Meagan Jones, Jana Zawadzki, Diane Radford, Mesha Maren, M. Randal O'Wain, Saja Montague, Kati Grimmett, Chris Oxley, Giancarlo DiTrapano, Amanda Noa, Megan Butler, Blake Butler, Ashleigh Bryant Phillips, Joseph Grantham, Nicolette Polek, Jordan Castro, Chelsea Martin, Amanda McNeil, Elle Nash, and Daisuke Shen (thank you also for the fact about fireflies), and all my friends in church basements and

Zoom rooms. My friendships with you all have been one of the greatest gifts of my life.

Thank you for the early feedback and reads: Diane, Saja, Nicolette, Jordan, Chelsea, Daisuke, Lauren Lauterhahn, Jenny Offill, Halle Butler, Elizabeth Ellen, and Tao Lin. An especially big thank-you to Scott, Mesha, and Blake, whose insight and care helped shape this book.

Thank you to the publications and editors (Jordan, Michael Seidlinger, Chris Dankland, MaroVerlag, Martin Brinkmann, and Adam Gnade) who published these stories in their earlier forms.

Thank you to the Giancarlo DiTrapano Foundation for the Arts, for the support and magic, especially to Catherine Foulkrod and Giuseppe Avallone.

And, just to annoy Scott, I would like to thank my dog Jelly. Thanks, Jelly.

PREVIOUSLY PUBLISHED

"Dust Particles": *40 Likely to Die Before 40: An Introduction to Alt Lit* (out of print); German edition of *Black Cloud*
"The Ryans": *X-R-A-Y Literary Magazine*
"Roadkill": *Tyrant Magazine*
"Nicole Took Her Shirt Off First": *Sundog Lit*; German edition of *Black Cloud*
"Same Person, Different Fires": *Hello America* (audio only)

© Saja Montague

JULIET ESCORIA is the author of the novel *Juliet the Maniac*, which was named a best book of the year by *Nylon*, *Elle*, *BuzzFeed*, and other publications and was short-listed for the VCU Cabell First Novelist Award. She also wrote the poetry collection *Witch Hunt* and the story collection *Black Cloud*, which were both listed in various best-of-the-year roundups. Her writing can be found in such publications as *Prelude*, *VICE*, *Fader*, *BOMB*, and *The New York Times* and has been translated into many languages. She was born in Australia and raised in San Diego, and currently lives in West Virginia, where she teaches English at a community college.